W9-BDC-219

I.S. 61 Library

Also by Denise Lewis Patrick:

The Adventures of Midnight Son

THE LONGEST RIDE

DENISE LEWIS PATRICK

THE LONGEST RIDE

Henry Holt and Company ★ New York

Henry Holt and Company, LLC
Publishers since 1866
115 West 18th Street
New York, New York 10011
Henry Holt is a registered trademark of Henry Holt and Company, LLC

Copyright © 1999 by Denise Lewis Patrick
All rights reserved.
Published in Canada by Fitzhenry & Whiteside Ltd.,
195 Allstate Parkway, Markham, Ontario L3R 4T8.

Library of Congress Cataloging-in-Publication Data
Patrick, Denise Lewis.
    The longest ride / Denise Lewis Patrick.
        p.   cm.
    Sequel to: The adventures of Midnight Son.
    Summary: At the end of the Civil War, Midnight, a fourteen-year-old
black cowboy and runaway slave who nurtures the dream of being
reunited with his family, finds his destiny linked with that of two
Arapaho Indians.
    1. Afro-Americans—Juvenile fiction. [1. Afro-Americans—
Fiction. 2. Cowboys—Fiction. 3. Frontier and pioneer life—West
(U.S.)—Fiction. 4. West (U.S.)—Fiction. 5. Arapaho Indians—
Fiction. 6. Indians of North America—Great Plains—Fiction.]   I. Title.
PZ7.P2747Lo   1999   [Fic]—dc21   98-54828

ISBN 0-8050-4715-8/First Edition—1999
Printed in the United States of America on acid-free paper. ∞
10   9   8   7   6   5   4   3   2   1

For my family—
the one I was born into,
and the one I chose through friendship
                    —D. L. P.

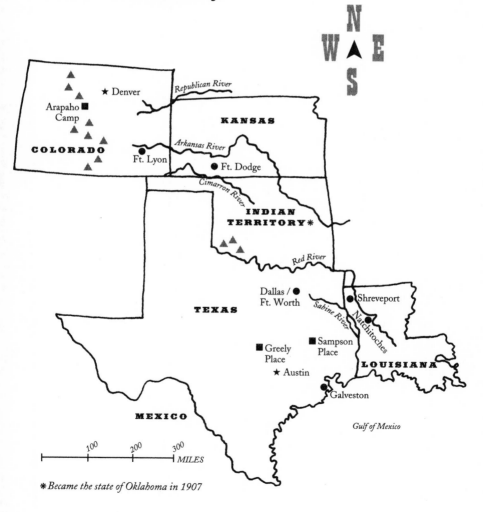

Midnight's Journey to Find His Family

N **W** ▲ **E** **S**

COLORADO

★ Denver

Arapaho ■ Camp

Republican River

KANSAS

Arkansas River

● Ft. Lyon

● Ft. Dodge

Cimarron River

INDIAN TERRITORY✱

Red River

TEXAS

Dallas / ● Ft. Worth

● Shreveport

Sabine River

Natchitoches

■ Greely Place

■ Sampson Place

LOUISIANA

★ Austin

● Galveston

MEXICO

Gulf of Mexico

100   200   300
├───┼───┼───┤ *MILES*

✱ *Became the state of Oklahoma in 1907*

THE LONGEST RIDE

1

The cool spring weather had turned downright cold. Two riders trotted along the rocky road halfway between Denver and Fort Lyon. From a distance, they seemed to be grown men, riding tall and broad shouldered in their saddles. Suddenly one of them let out a loud whoop in a boy's voice, and the race was on.

"You're gonna eat some dust this time, Louis Holt!" A grinning boy with skin the color of black coffee leaned toward his horse's neck, urging the animal into a full gallop. He loosened the reins and pulled a full horse's length ahead. Coming up fast was a laughing, suntanned older boy with a long chin and flying brown hair chopped to his ears.

"Try and make me, Midnight Son!" he shouted.

Midnight was nearly fifteen, Louis—Lou Boy—only

seventeen. They were young, and their trip had been long. Now that the rest station was close, they just wanted to break out and have some fun. After all, the Rocky Mountains were spread wide behind them, and the open plains rolled out ahead like a grassy green river flowing to the edge of the world.

Midnight Son whispered breathlessly into his horse's ears. "Come on, Dahomey . . . I'm gonna beat Lou Boy today!" He bent until his nose brushed Dahomey's black mane, digging his heels into the animal's flanks. One hand held tight to the worn felt hat pulled over his thick hair. Midnight's whole body was set on winning.

Lou Boy's brown mare was up for a fight. She ran hard past them.

"Let's go, Buttercup!" Lou Boy yelled, slapping her flank with his own wide-brimmed hat. But Dahomey began to inch up nose to nose with Buttercup. Then he edged past to take a tight lead. He stretched the lead out—by a nose, then by a head, and finally, by a length.

"Yo!" Midnight cried, bouncing up in his saddle and twisting back to grin. "We did it! We did it!" He snatched the hat off his woolly head and waved it in the air.

Lou Boy didn't look a bit upset. He watched Midnight prancing Dahomey around and laughed. "Looks like ya beat me for sure this time!"

"Looks like you're right, Lou Boy!" Midnight shot back.

He pulled himself up tall in his saddle. If he'd stuck his chest out any more, the shiny silver buttons on his new denim waistcoat would have popped right off. The cowboys slowed their horses to a trot.

Midnight finally broke the quietness. "Lou Boy, I got somethin' to tell ya."

Lou Boy's sharp blue eyes narrowed under bushy dark brows. "Don't sound like nothin' I might wanna hear, now, do it?"

"My folks and my sisters are on my mind all the time. Even in my dreams. I been thinkin' real hard about this, and—"

"And?" Lou Boy blurted out.

"I'm not goin' back to the ranch with y'all. When we get to the station, I'm tellin' Joe B. that I'm headin' back to that plantation in Texas to rescue my folks." As he said the words, Midnight took in a long, deep breath. He had really, truly decided.

"There's a Civil War goin' on, or did you forget?" Lou Boy blustered.

"War or no—my mind's set. They helped me escape. I can't let them put up with one more day or one more hour as somebody's property!" Midnight felt excited, like he always did at the beginning of a new trail drive. He felt strong. Unafraid.

Lou Boy smiled slowly. "I always had a feelin' that you would come to this idea, Midnight. You got a plan?"

Midnight snorted. "Well, I'm not *beggin'* for their

freedom, and I certainly ain't gonna pay for it. 'Sides that, no—I ain't worked out a plan yet."

With that, they traveled on a few miles deep in thought, chased and surrounded by puffs of dust. The dust made Midnight think of west Texas and the Crazy Eight ranch. That's where he'd met Lou Boy.

He'd ridden out on his first cattle drive from the Crazy Eight a year and a half ago. Joe B. Martin, the owner, had hired Midnight on as horse wrangler. He'd spent half a year in Mexico before that, learning roping and riding and just about everything he needed to know from a Mexican cowboy, a *gaucho*. It was a wonder that Midnight had ended up in Mexico in the first place. After all, he'd been a runaway slave, just a kid, traveling alone. Anything could've happened to him. He knew that many runaways weren't so lucky. Midnight shook his head, trying to shake away the scary memory.

Lou Boy raised one eyebrow. "Don't you know lookin' back is a dangerous thing?"

"Lou Boy, I'm colored and I'm a runaway slave. For me, *livin'* is a dangerous thing."

They rode way past dark, trying to push the horses on to the station. A raiding party of Sioux and Cheyenne warriors had attacked a wagon train along this trail just a week ago. Soldiers from the fort had been posted at the rest station to protect travelers. Tonight a cloudy sky and a hidden moon made them stop and strike camp near some flat rocks a few yards away from the main road.

Midnight fell asleep as soon as he wrapped his Mexican blanket around his shoulders. He tossed and turned on the hard, cold ground. Then the nightmare came, the same nightmare he'd had every few nights for the past year. The dream swooped down on him like a hungry owl.

Clouds. In the dream dark, gray clouds swirled around him. He was five—maybe six years old. On the plantation.

"Midnight! Midnight!" A small voice sounded far away. Suddenly something jerked Midnight through the clouds. Now he was holding his older sister, Lady's, outstretched hand. He could see her egg-shaped face as plain as day. She was wide-eyed. Her left cheek twitched a little, the way it always did when she was scared. Her fingers squeezed his.

"Midnight! Midnight!" Lady was pulling away from him. Midnight tried to hold her hand tighter, but she was slipping away.

"SOLD!" A thundering voice roared from nowhere.

"MIDNIGHT! HELP ME!" Lady's little-girl screams bounced around the thundering voice. Midnight tried to reach out, tried to catch her. But he felt himself moving farther and farther away. . . . "MIDNIGHT! MIDNIGHT!"

"NOOOO!" Midnight wailed. He fell to the ground. His face was covered with dirt and tears. "Noooo!"

She was gone. The clouds sucked her up and Lady was gone.

★   ★   ★

"Midnight! Wake up! Wake up!" Lou Boy was shaking him hard. Midnight sat bolt upright, blinking at Lou Boy.

"My sister—," Midnight began, then stopped.

Lady had been sold away from the rest of the family when she was ten years old. They never saw her again. Midnight hadn't forgotten. He pushed Lou Boy away, trying to tuck his pain out of sight.

"It's that dream again, right? You never get a decent night's sleep anymore."

"Just never mind." Midnight looked down at the blue-and-yellow pattern woven into his blanket.

"But you were a *kid*! You couldn't stop what happened."

"Tell that to my nightmare!" Midnight shouted, beating the ground with his fist.

As Lou Boy backed off to the campfire, Midnight hunched under the blanket. He figured Lou Boy would leave him alone. After all, Lou Boy knew quite a lot about bad dreams himself. He had watched his own father die, sucked away by a twister on a cattle drive.

By the time the sun rose, they'd had strong black coffee and picked up the trail without much conversation. It was getting colder.

The change in the air made Midnight shiver. He wiggled his shoulders inside the buckskin jacket he'd bought in Denver with some of his pay. He was always careful not to spend all his money at once the way some of the cowboys did. They always kidded him about it, saying that he must have a sweetheart somewhere. Why else would a lonesome young cowpoke save all his money? Midnight never answered them. In his heart, he knew that one day he would need that money. And when he did, he was going to have it.

After much silence Midnight broke the ice.

"Lou Boy, sorry I—"

"Like you said last night, never mind."

Midnight changed the subject.

"Feels right like winter, don't it?"

"Sure does. This ain't April weather no more."

"Well, I'll be lookin' for a warm fire at that stage station. Can't be much longer, huh?"

"Naw—one or two hours at most. We're lucky Joe B. don't mind us havin' a little time for ourselves. Shucks, we just spent four months drivin' ornery longhorns all the way from Texas up here to Fort Lyon for them soldiers."

"Yeah, dodgin' Cheyenne dog soldiers all the way. I hear them Indians are some fierce fighters," Midnight said. He turned as he spoke. The distant foothills behind them seemed empty—until a young deer strolled out from some scraggly cottonwood trees. If deer were going about their business, no humans were nearby. He turned back to Lou Boy.

"Joe B. is a fair boss. He gives us our due. And man, was this trip worth it. I never seen the likes of Denver before. All the folks. All the shops. It sure is a wonder. But that noise!"

Lou Boy laughed. "Guess you'll never be a city boy, Midnight."

Midnight was about to give a smart answer when an unexpectedly icy wind blasted his face, bringing tears to his eyes. The northern sky was filling with gray clouds.

2

Lou Boy was already turned to the flat storm clouds rolling their way. The wind whipped his hair across most of his face, so Midnight couldn't see it. His jaw was pulled tight. He suddenly spurred Buttercup roughly, sending her into a wild gallop.

"Lou Boy, slow down!" Midnight and Dahomey took out after them. "Lou Boy! Think! This ain't a twister!" Small white flecks began blowing around them.

"Clear your head, Louis Holt!" Midnight's lips were fighting the deepening cold. "This ain't the roarin', spinnin' madness of that tornado."

"It took my pa, Midnight. Swept him up like a twig! Wasn't nothin' left of him or his horse."

"We both tried to fight that wind, Lou Boy. You know it was useless. Big Lou was just gone."

"You got your nightmares, I got mine!" Lou Boy yelled. "I dream about Pa all the time. Folks keep sayin'

I'm a man, I should get on with my life. Midnight, I ain't *got* no life, except riding this blasted trail!"

Midnight pressed his spurs into Dahomey's flanks. Steam shot out of his nostrils. Snow was swirling down faster. The flakes were bigger. The ground was already covered with a thick white powder. Midnight blinked as wet snow fell onto his eyelashes. As he got closer he reached over and grabbed Buttercup's reins, pulling back to slow her down.

"Here!" Midnight pushed the reins toward Lou Boy's hands. "Take Buttercup back!"

Midnight spoke more gently. "Believe me, I know what it feels like to be alone. 'Specially when you didn't choose it."

Lou Boy shuddered, then took control of his horse. He shook his head. "That ain't true, you know. Ma died when I was six years old. Then Pa back in Kansas. Now I ain't got a blood relative on this earth. *You* got a whole family somewhere."

"You're right, Lou Boy, and that's a fact. I'll make a bargain with you. You listenin'?"

Lou Boy cocked his head to one side.

"I am."

"You keep on tellin' me the truth. Always. No matter what I say. No matter what nobody else says. I'll do the same for you. Let's count on each other like family. No matter what nobody else says. Deal?" Midnight looked straight into Lou Boy's eyes.

"Deal," Lou Boy said, without hesitating.

★ ★ ★

The blizzard was upon them. Sharp, powerful cold burned their faces and stung their fingers through their gloves. Dahomey and Buttercup strained to lift their hooves in the packed snow. It was showering down like heavy rain. Everything around them was white.

"W-What can we do?" Midnight called out. "Pretty soon our horses will be up to their knees in snow!"

"Got to find shelter! No use tryin' to get to the station!" Lou Boy yelled back. "Let's stay close!"

"If it gets much worse, we'll haveta hold a rope between us to keep together!"

The wind whistled, taking the sounds of their voices away with it. Midnight tried to shake the snow from his face, but it was sticking just like it was everywhere else. He could barely see a dozen paces beyond Dahomey's nose. Without warning, Dahomey stood still.

"H-Hey! Come on, boy! L-Let's go! C-Can't s-s-stop here!" It was so cold, Midnight didn't want to use the spurs. He tried to let up his grip on the reins. Dahomey only shook his head and stood, pawing in the snow. Midnight climbed out of the saddle. He could still make out the darkness of Lou Boy's back through the gusts of white powder.

"Lou B-Boy!" Midnight's throat was dry and tight. He couldn't get more than a hoarse whisper out. He pulled Dahomey's reins over the horse's head. At first Dahomey refused to follow, because he couldn't see where he was going. But they had to keep on, even if Midnight dragged Dahomey.

"All w-we b-been through, D-Dahomey . . . d-desert with n-no water, f-floods, t-t-twister. . . . C-C-Can't let n-no b-blizzard . . . s-stop us. . . ." Midnight trudged on, trying to keep the horse moving. Trying to keep himself moving. He was freezing.

After a while, Midnight looked up for Lou Boy. All he could see was whiteness.

"L-Lou Boy!"

It was perfectly quiet around him. Even his own steps made no noise as he plowed through the snow.

Suddenly, his toe slammed against something hard—a rock hidden under the snow. Dahomey balked, jerking his head back and snatching the reins out of Midnight's hands. Midnight lost his balance and flew headfirst down a steep snowbank. With a muffled thump, he crumpled against a tree trunk. The force of his weight shook the small tree. Clumps of snow dropped from the upper branches, covering Midnight's body.

He was stunned. He had hit his head and landed with his knees bent and his legs twisted beneath him. He pushed up dizzily onto his elbows and tried to stand. Pain shot through his right foot and ankle. Midnight slumped back.

"Lou Boy? D-Dahomey!" he croaked out to the wind. Midnight closed his eyes for a moment, then looked up the slope rising over him. He had fallen quite a way. No telling how soon Lou Boy would notice that he was missing. And there was no telling where Dahomey was.

After a little while, Midnight sat up. When his head

stopped throbbing, he began scooping snow off himself. The snow had stopped falling now, but the wind was still swirling powdery flakes from the trees. The cold had made his fingers stiff. He clutched them into fists and pulled to his knees.

I'll crawl, he thought. He started to drag himself along the ground. Each time the leg bumped, even slightly, pain ran like a bolt of lightning through his foot and ankle. He pulled himself a few feet and stopped, panting.

Midnight sat on his rear and tried to rub his hands along his arms. He needed to rest. Just a bit of rest. . . . As he struggled to keep his eyes open, the cold seemed to cover him like a warm blanket.

Just then a shadow appeared in the white fog. Midnight thought he was dreaming.

"L-Lou B-Boy?" Midnight whispered. One dark shape came toward him, then another. They were wrapped in shaggy buffalo skin robes that covered their heads and swept down to the snowy ground. Against the white background he could see the dark, taut strings of the long bows they held. Two gleaming arrow tips were pointing down. Midnight tried to make out the details of their faces. Hoods hid their features, but not the black hair blowing out from underneath. They were Indians.

Midnight had heard many stories from other cowboys at the Crazy Eight and in the towns they'd passed through about "bloodthirsty Injuns" and "murdering red men." Yet the one Indian he'd really known was a hardworking man like any other.

Soon the men were standing over him, staring. One of the men spoke two or three words in his own language. The other shook his head and grunted. They seemed to disagree. They fired a few more words at each other. Then one of them lifted Midnight carefully. He couldn't—and didn't—try to fight them. Nearby were two horses. The men put him onto one, with its rider climbing up behind. The warmth of the buffalo robe and another human body seemed to pull Midnight's strength clean away. He passed out.

3

Midnight's eyes flickered. He was in dim light inside a tipi. Heaps of soft buffalo skin blankets surrounded him. In the center of the floor a fire burned in a hole in the ground. A flash of daylight entered the tipi as part of the wall across from him opened up.

Next he saw a girl's face. It was brown and red at the same time, like polished mahogany. Not at all what Midnight expected. She stuck her head into the tipi, two thick black braids swinging across her chest. She smiled at Midnight. Her bright white teeth made him think of the snow. Then Lou Boy and Dahomey . . .

The girl walked in silently, bringing a water pouch. The straight deerskin dress she wore had rows of tiny beads sewn around the neck and down the center, making a pattern of birds and stars.

"You must drink," she said in a clear voice.

Midnight almost jumped. The hunters who found him

had talked in their own language. He never thought to hear English in their camp. The girl stopped an arm's length away, holding out the water pouch. As he reached to take it, his head pounded.

"Thanks," he croaked.

She watched him gulp the water. He wondered how long he'd been here. He stopped mid-drink and looked down at himself. His clothes—the nice new vest he'd bought in Denver, the new pants, the boots Juan Diego had given him back in Mexico—all gone. He was wearing only his flannel shirt and his underwear.

"My duds!" he shouted, grabbing up the buffalo skin to cover himself. "Where in tarnation are my clothes?"

The girl laughed. "Dry, now," she said, waving her hand toward the wall behind him. Two forked poles were stuck in the ground. A third pole rested crosswise in the forks, making a clothesline. All of Midnight's things were hanging up. His boots stood nearby, along with his hat. Everything was clean and dry.

Midnight grinned sheepishly. "Common sense oughta tell me that my duds woulda been soaked through from layin' in that snow." He cleared his throat. "Mind if I get dressed?" She passed him his pants and slipped out of the tipi. He managed to pull them on, but the dull ache at the back of his head throbbed. He eased onto the buffalo skins.

"I'm Midnight Son," he said when she appeared again.

"I am Winter Mary."

"Where did you get your name—" They spoke at the same time, surprising themselves and each other.

"You have an Indian name," Winter Mary said as she studied Midnight's face. She was looking at him as if she could find out all about his life through his eyes. He knew that some people could do that, like Mississippi Slim, his best friend when he started at the Crazy Eight.

"I was born at the stroke of midnight. My papa's first son. Was a slave back in Texas. Now I'm a cowpoke."

"Cow-poke?"

"You know, takin' care of horses and cattle."

"Ah. Ne'ina—my mother—is one of the dark people, like you. I have the name of her sister." She paused. "Many times I wish that I could know more about my mother's clan. She taught us—my father, my brother, me—your words. Your language. Not much more."

Midnight understood. "I reckon she don't talk much 'bout her past, huh?"

Winter Mary shook her head.

"My father's people found Ne'ina long ago in the Moon of Strong Cold. She had been a slave to settlers in a wagon train coming from the East. There was a storm. She was young and hurt, like you. They were lost for many sleeps in the snow. One by one, all caught fever. Only my mother survived. It took many moons, but the Arapaho made her well. She stayed and became my father's wife."

The warmth of the tent and Winter Mary's voice had made Midnight sleepy again. He tried to shake it away.

"Winter Mary, I need to get outta here."

"Oh! I will help you get some air." Midnight threw the skins back and struggled to get to his feet.

"No, I mean *leave*. You know anything 'bout my friend? Anybody find him?"

"Friend?" She opened the flap. "No, just you," she said quietly. "There was no one else. If night had come while you were lost, you would surely have met the Great Spirit. My brother, Eagle Eye, brought you here two sleeps ago."

Outside, the warm weather was coming back quickly after the unexpected storm. Two skinny dogs ran between some melting patches of snow. The bright sun had already begun to dry the muddy ground. What Midnight saw surprised him.

The camp was a small rough clearing near the foothills of the mountains. There were only three other tipis, one larger than the others. They were patched and worn. A couple of lean-tos had been set up against the rocks, animal hides stretched and staked into the ground to keep out wind, rain, and snow.

"This here's an odd spot for a camp, ain't it?" Midnight noticed that no enemy could get in easy, with the rocks on three sides. That meant the Indians couldn't get out easy, either.

"Well—" Winter Mary stopped talking. She let go of Midnight so suddenly that he nearly fell to the ground. He caught himself.

"Hey, Winter Mary!"

"This is Big Running Fox. My father," she said. Midnight looked past her to see an Indian man. Was he one of the two from the woods? No, he seemed taller.

"You are not hurt badly." He looked hard at Midnight with sharp eyes. "Nothing broken. Where were you headed?"

Big Running Fox did not sit, kneel, or even squat. He stood straight as a tree trunk and looked down his nose. Winter Mary helped Midnight sit. He had no choice but to look up at the wide-chested man.

"I was on my way from Denver to Fort Lyon," Midnight said truthfully. "How far off the trail am I now?"

Big Running Fox ignored Midnight's question, frowning. "You have business with bluecoats?"

"Bluecoats?" Midnight repeated. He watched the sunlight bounce off the metal-studded belt slung around Big Running Fox's hip. The carved bone handle of a large bowie knife jutted out from it. Midnight decided to keep telling the straight truth.

"It was my boss who had the business," he said. "We delivered a herd of cattle to the fort. After, my partner and me took a side trip to see the sights in Denver. We were aimin' to head back to Texas from Fort Lyon in a couple of days with the rest of our crew."

"So you and your Texas people feed our enemies while they starve Arapaho."

"No! All I want is my horse—"

Big Running Fox cut his words off. "Maybe you don't

speak the truth. Maybe bluecoats pay you for more than cattle. Maybe they pay you for information about Indians. You have seen my camp. We cannot let you go to the fort!" He spun on his heel and walked away.

Midnight's heart thumped. Winter Mary was gone, and he wondered what Big Running Fox would do next.

4

With a closer look, Midnight could see that the camp looked as though it had been thrown up in a hurry. The grass between the tents wasn't cleared away, only trampled down. The buildings made a tight circle at the bottom of a steep, rocky hill. In the center, some women were tending the hindquarter of a small buck as it roasted over a fire. Two old men sat smoking a pipe. Some little children were playing a game.

Midnight looked for horses. Besides the two dogs, he hadn't seen any other animals. He strained to hear something—anything—behind the great silence. He pushed himself up to stand.

"Boy child!" Startled, Midnight turned too quickly, twisting his foot again. A sharp pain sliced across his ankle.

A small dark brown woman with a crown of curly black hair shot her body out of a lean-to. She was not Indian.

She wore a long deerskin shirt over a huge, faded blue cotton skirt that fell to her ankles. He could see moccasins underneath. Slung around her waist was a belt of hammered flat silver circles strung together on a leather cord. Layers of beads were roped around her neck. A long hairpin made from some sort of animal bone held the wiry front hair away from her eyes. She motioned to him.

"Boy child, you got bruises, bumps, ankle nearly broke. Why you walking about? Come back to the tipi." She took his elbow to turn him around.

"Naw, I'm really all right." Midnight tried to pull away, but her grip was strong. He slumped a little and gave in. She guided him in the direction of the old men. They had comfortable-looking stools covered with soft buffalo hair. There was an empty one, and she sat him down on it, raising his foot gently and propping it up on a nearby rock. She worked the boot off carefully, but it hurt just the same. After she closely examined the bandage, she squatted, facing him.

"Tellin' tales don't suit you, Midnight Son. Why not rest awhile?" Except for tiny wrinkles around her eyes, her face was smooth and young looking. She had a dark blue circle tattooed right in the center of her wide forehead. A long scar curved from her cheek to her left ear. Midnight had seen scars like that many times. He wondered if she had gotten it when she was a slave.

"They call me Raven Woman, mother to Winter Mary and Eagle Eye. Winter Mary has a fine gift for reading people. She tells me you're an honest man. Now, is she right?" When she spoke Winter Mary's name, Raven Woman turned around as if her daughter was near. Midnight followed her eyes to a break between the tipis. Winter Mary and another girl appeared, carrying bundles of firewood to lay under the roasting deer. Midnight's eyes met Winter Mary's.

"I raised her more American than Arapaho. Her pa says she talks too much for an Indian girl. She already told me all 'bout *you*."

"Me? Look, Miss Raven Woman, the whole entire truth is I'm on my way to help my folks escape bondage. I just want my horse so I can leave."

Raven Woman was looking at him curiously with her arms folded.

"I feel for you, boy child. You miss your family. But . . ." She shook her head. "Horses are scarce now. Arapaho most likely will not return your horse. I'll see what I can do."

"Please? I ain't got nothin' to do with the army. How come Big Runnin' Fox don't trust what I say?"

Raven Woman picked up a stick and drew a wiggly line in the drying mud. "Trust is like this stick, Midnight—it can be broken easy."

Raven Woman didn't look at him, but kept her eyes on the stick as she twirled it between her fingers and talked.

"I was born in Missouri. Never knew my own ma or pa. They got sold away from us like my brothers. Me and my sister were left alone. Then they sold me away. My sister's face is still clear in my head after all these years. I named my girl, Mary, after her. I ended up with the Arapaho." She paused.

"Big Runnin' Fox and me raised good children. We lived good. When the soldiers came, buildin' forts, things changed. They wanted us on reservations. We want to stay free. So we keep moving our camps. Last November we camped with Cheyenne—at a place called Sand Creek. Hunting was very bad there, so our warriors went far to hunt buffalo. One sunrise while the warriors were gone, bluecoats swarmed upon us like hornets. The Cheyenne leader, Black Kettle, tried to talk to them. He showed papers—a treaty. They shot him down." She stopped, not lifting her head. Though her voice did not change, Midnight saw big tears dropping from her face onto the ground.

"They kept shooting. We ran. I pushed Winter Mary ahead of me. A soldier leaned from his horse and hit me with his sword." She traced the curve of the scar on her face with the stick.

"I stumbled, but I grabbed my child and we ran for our lives. We left our hurt and dead." She raised her eyes. "See what trust did for us, Midnight Son."

Midnight's insides began to ache. In his mind's eye, he could picture it.

"So it's all a big lie, that the army is tryin' to find a place for you?"

"Bluecoats want to *own* the land!" An angry young man's voice interrupted. "They push us and push us. If they could, they would push all our nations off the edge of the world!"

A long shadow fell across them. Midnight squinted and looked up. Something about this young warrior seemed familiar.

"Here is my son, Eagle Eye." Raven Woman's voice changed from sadness to pride.

Midnight took a close look at Winter Mary's brother. His eyes were angry fireballs over sharp cheekbones. Skin dark brown and shining. He was taller than his mother and sister, big and barrel-chested like his father. His heavy black hair was wavy at the top of his head, parted into two braids flowing past his shoulders. He held his head high.

"All we want is to live as our ancestors did. Following our own ways. Bluecoats fear us because they don't like different. So we must fight them just to live. Now they leave us no choice. We must destroy them or they will destroy us!" His voice was deep. His chest heaved as he spoke. Midnight looked from the mother's face to her son's.

So this is it, he thought. *They ain't startin' the fightin', they're fightin' back. The army don't really want peace. They want this land, clear of trees, of buffalo—and especially Indians. They're killin' innocent people to get ahold of this land. This ain't the story that's gettin' told.*

Anger boiled up inside Midnight. At that moment, his family, Lou Boy, and Dahomey were far back in his mind.

"You say you are not with the bluecoats. Prove it."

Eagle Eye clenched his jaw. Midnight struggled to get to his feet. He was chin to chin with Eagle Eye.

"Just what is it that you want me to do?" Midnight questioned as he boldly stared at Eagle Eye.

"Ride to the Republican River, south of Denver. Then four days east. Our people are camped near the north fork of the river. Tell them that Big Running Fox and his clan are trapped here. You will pass the soldiers without being stopped."

"Why, 'cause I'm not Indian?"

"You *will* do this! We cannot afford to lose more braves."

"You sayin' that you saved my life just to use me in your war?"

"WE WILL NOT BE DESTROYED!" Eagle Eye's entire body trembled as he shouted. Midnight felt the hair on his neck bristle. He had been ready to help them move, ready to help them fight, even. But to travel deep into Indian Territory, maybe with soldiers on his tail—not knowing if or when he'd get back—that was hard to agree to.

"Now, listen here, Eagle Eye. I know 'bout bein' destroyed. Slave masters destroy slaves little by little, day by day. I don't want *my* family destroyed, either. That's why I'm on my way to get 'em. If you tryin' to tell me that my people ain't as important as yours . . ."

Eagle Eye lunged at Midnight. Midnight bobbed out of the way. Raven Woman jumped up to her toes. Her eyes only reached the brave's chin, but he stepped back.

"Eagle Eye! Let Midnight Son go. Now I find out that you didn't set out to save a human life. You saved him only to get a body to throw to the bluecoats. Are you just like them?"

Eagle Eye's eyes widened in horror. He opened his mouth, but nothing came out. His eyes darted to Midnight, then to his mother. Midnight could tell that Raven Woman's words had made Eagle Eye think in a way he hadn't before.

"Ne'ina," he sputtered. "I—" He seemed unsure of what to say next. He cut a look at Midnight, eyeing him from his feet up to his head. "I must go." His nose flared a little, then he brushed by Midnight roughly, almost knocking him down.

Raven Woman touched Midnight's arm.

"My son cannot feel another's pain now. But try to remember that his heart—like yours—is first with his people."

5

Raven Woman headed slowly toward the cooking fire with her head bent. The old men shuffled off behind Eagle Eye. Two other braves and another older warrior ducked into a tipi at the far end of the camp. Big Running Fox must have been inside already. Midnight didn't move. He couldn't.

He felt wiped out. There had been too many words. Too many feelings. When he thought of Winter Mary and Raven Woman, he felt sorry that life had led them to this scary place. They might never get out. He could even understand Eagle Eye's anger.

"Midnight Son?" Midnight jumped nervously. He spun around to stare at Winter Mary as if she might be reading his mind. But she only smiled.

"You have not eaten. A man must have strength to recover from injuries. Come." She took his arm like her mother had done. Midnight looked over at the largest tipi just long enough to see Eagle Eye rush out, followed by his father. They passed angry words, then the young brave ducked between the tipis. Seconds later, Midnight could hear horse hooves speeding away from the camp. He felt relieved. *Eagle Eye must've hit the trail to deliver that message himself.*

As Winter Mary saw her brother leave, a tiny flicker of worry passed over her face. Midnight felt he should say something. He took a deep breath.

"Winter Mary?"

"Yes?"

The words fell out, one on top of the other. "Before this happened, I'd set my mind to go directly for my folks. War and all—nothin' really matters to me no more except them. I know I can't truly enjoy bein' free if they ain't, too."

Winter Mary's eyes filled with tears.

"At first I thought Eagle Eye should ask you to help us. Now I see that it is not fair. You have a different life journey." They had walked the few paces to the big tipi.

"It is good to be sure of your journey," she said thoughtfully. She raised the tipi flap and slipped inside.

Midnight frowned, feeling very uneasy.

He followed Winter Mary inside. He didn't let himself think about his decision any more.

Big Running Fox sat in the center of a small circle of men near a fire pit.

"Midnight Son!" Big Running Fox motioned. "Come, sit here." Midnight moved slowly to a space across from one of the men he'd seen outside. Big Running Fox's eyes moved with him. The men had been talking quietly until Midnight came among them. Now they were silent as Raven Woman and Winter Mary served food.

Raven Woman leaned to give Big Running Fox a wooden cup filled with a warm drink. Midnight could smell the strong mint tea. He gathered his nerve and spoke up.

"You're breakin' bread with me? I don't mean no disrespect, but where I come from we don't sit to table with somebody we hardly trust!"

Big Running Fox nodded.

"That is the way it should be. No man should eat with an enemy. I sent for you, Midnight Son, because my closed mind is now opened. These elders, and others"—he paused and his eyes rested on Raven Woman—"have shared their wisdom with me. They tell me you have one purpose to your travel, to unite your family. This is a worthy cause."

"So now you believe that I'm not workin' with the bluecoats?"

"Yes."

Midnight's heart skipped a beat. "Then I can have my horse and get on my way?" He began to push up off the floor, then remembered that he'd been *asked* to eat. He looked at Winter Mary. She didn't move her body at all, but drew her eyebrows together. Midnight eased back down.

Big Running Fox shifted in his seat and fingered one of the many rows of beads hanging around his neck. He spoke slowly.

"It seems that the young bear is not grateful to be sprung from his trap, my brothers." A grumble of agreement surrounded Midnight.

Big Running Fox added, "It was we who voted against Eagle Eye's plan to have you ransom yourself. We could not agree to such a plan."

Midnight's cheeks flushed hot with shame.

"It don't seem like I'm grateful. But I am. It's just that—well, a dream is leadin' me."

"Dreams are strong winds sent from the Great Spirit," Big Running Fox said quietly. "You cannot control the wind."

Winter Mary placed a bowl in front of Midnight. Its wonderful smell pulled his hand to the wooden spoon. He settled down to eat slowly, enjoying the thick, meaty stew. He bit into crunchy green beans and tender hunks of meat. Probably some of the deer he'd seen the women roasting before.

"And now, Midnight Son. I have saved a memory for you." Big Running Fox lit a long pipe. Like most older men Midnight had known, Big Running Fox seemed to feel that eating, drinking, and telling stories belonged together. He stared at the fire as he started talking, as if he were calling the words and pictures and feelings up out of the smoky past.

"I was a young boy. Not even a brave," Big Running Fox began. "Yet I cried like a pup to my elders to go out on the buffalo hunt. My father knew that only the Great Spirit could show me my right place and time on this earth. So he let me have my way.

"Once the leaders sighted the herd, we made small fires this way"—Big Running Fox drew a wide circle in the air with his hands—"around the animals. Buffalo will not cross fire," he explained to Midnight.

"Some braves rubbed themselves with mud to cover their man scent. The animals backed away from the fire, becoming confused. Then the hunters who were outside the ring on horseback could take aim.

"When the smoke and dust began to rise, I caught sight of a great shaggy bull halfway across the ring. I raced my pony along the rim of the circle, weaving in and out among the experienced braves. My pony was not prepared for the thunder of the hooves and the angry bellowing of the trapped buffalo.

"He skidded to a stop. I looked up and saw the flashing eyes through the flames. The bull—*my bull*—soared through the ring of fire in a horrible cloud of anger!

"I wondered, 'What kind of demon beast is this that flies through fire unafraid?' With one butt of his mighty head, my bow flew one way, I another. The bull stood over me. One of the horns was broken, so I knew this was a fierce warrior. I can still remember the smell—of my own fear.

"All my proud, boastful thoughts ran out of me into the ground. The animal looked at me and saw my foolishness. He curled his lip and snorted. Then he tossed his head and heaved his great body clear of me."

Midnight hadn't taken a bite while Big Running Fox was speaking.

"You mean to say that buffalo laughed at you? He could well have run them horns right through you!"

"Let me tell all. That was my first hunt. Some seasons later I was sent with two braves to trade with the Cheyenne. I saw through some trees a small group of buffalo, one bull with several cows and calves. Though I was older, I was still full of false pride. I had planned to show off my skills as a hunter, if I got the chance. And here it was! I drew an arrow and approached with my bow. That was when I saw the broken horn.

"I knew it was the same bull. Knowing that we could bring him down, I called to my friends. My people could surely use the meat, and this time I would win the battle. The bull bellowed a warning to the other animals and charged at me. I let fly one arrow and another. None touched him! He kept coming.

"I pulled my horse out of his path and circled to come at him again, when he stopped and stood still.

"I took aim, but the bull did not move. I held my arrow in puzzlement. Then I saw from the corner of my eye that the small herd was far away now. The bull snorted and turned away after them."

Midnight leaned toward Big Running Fox. "And then? What happened?"

"I put away my bow."

"You had him, then! Three of ya, and you just rode away?" Midnight narrowed his eyes. "Seems like that bull was thinkin' more like a man than you. First, he wouldn't kill a kid. Then he used you to save his herd. Takin' him down just for sport would be wrong."

"I have come to understand that no creature is of any more or less worth than another. This idea was never clear to me until that day. The bull had spared my life once. I now had a chance to spare his—and more. Proving myself as a hunter could wait. I had to make a choice in the moment. I think I made the right one."

Midnight knew they weren't talking about a bull and a young brave anymore.

"Are you sayin' that what I'm doin' is wrong?" He jumped up, angry. "I thought you understood what I need to do for my people. You think you know what's right for me?"

"I cannot. Only you can know that. Just remember, the Great Spirit has given us one thing that we can keep in both life and death—honor."

Midnight was upset. He looked around for the first time and noticed that everyone else had left the tipi.

"Big Runnin' Fox, ain't there honor in wantin' my family to live free like me? Ain't there honor in wantin' to make it happen?"

"There is honor, too, in understanding the moment, Midnight Son." Big Running Fox reached into a pouch hanging beneath his beads and pulled something out. Dangling at the end of a leather string was a small buffalo carved of wood. Midnight held back for a minute, then leaned over to take it. He rolled it in his palm. It was warm in his hand. He hung it around his neck.

"Go now." Big Running Fox looked at Midnight hard for a moment, then dropped his eyes to the weakening fire.

Midnight knew there was no point in staying. He stormed out of the tipi into near darkness. His head ached and his thoughts were swirling inside.

A few minutes later, Winter Mary appeared. "Midnight, are you looking for your tipi?"

"No—I mean, yes. Your papa has me all mixed up." Midnight looked at her round face. For some reason, he wished that she would smile.

"I cannot stay. We are packing to move camp. My father tells me you will go at first light." Her eyes fell on the buffalo medallion. She reached quickly and touched it lightly with her fingers. "Safe journey, Midnight Son."

Midnight had no words. As Winter Mary blended into the night, he stumbled into the tipi and fell onto the buffalo skins. He lay awake for hours, turning things over in his mind. But he couldn't close his eyes, and he couldn't sleep.

6

Midnight's eyes fluttered. This time the dream was sudden and awful, as if a great dark cloth had been thrown over him. He fought it, waving his arms and kicking his legs. But the dream was heavy.

Fear blew over him like an icy wind. He was shaking. A faraway voice called out. "Midnight! Midnight!" Suddenly he felt his sister's hand squeezing his. He couldn't see her in the darkness. Couldn't even make out the shape of her small body. It was like holding on to a shadow.

"Midnight!" He clutched at her arm. *Where is she? Why can't I see her? Lady!* He stretched out both his hands, reaching, reaching. If only he could see her. Slowly the darkness began to brighten. There she was, a gray shape.

"Midnight!" she screamed, and turned to him. It wasn't Lady. It was Winter Mary! "Help me!" The freezing wind jerked her away, her long braids flying against his cheeks.

"Noooo!" Midnight moaned. He felt as if he were flying, spinning through snowflakes that stung his cheeks and sailing past charging, thundering buffalo. Faces rolled by. Lou Boy. Big Running Fox. Papa and Mama. Winter Mary was nodding and singing.

"Follow your heart. Heart never lies."

★   ★   ★

Midnight's eyes snapped wide open. The dream was different. It wasn't only about *his* family this time.

"That's it!" Midnight whispered to himself. Now that he was free, his world was bigger than just him, bigger than his family in Texas. *A free man's world is as big as everyone he meets. Now my world has Arapaho in it, and they need my help. I hope it ain't too late.* He grabbed his hat and rushed out of the tipi.

Daylight was on its way, but the sun wasn't up. Midnight rushed through the quiet camp. No one was out and about yet. The leftover roasting fire had burned down to a pile of glowing ashes. The rugged rocks curved around in a half circle behind him, rising up nearly twice as tall as he was. He headed across the camp past the council tipi, past skinny cottonwood trees stretching into woods that seemed to run downhill. He listened.

The horses were upwind. Midnight sighed with satisfaction. Then he tipped his head sideways and listened again. The faint sound of restless animals shifting their hooves came to him. He moved carefully behind the tipis, out of sight of the cooking fire. He took a quick look over his shoulder, then eased away from the tipis to stand close behind a young oak tree. Spring had already forced out the first leaves and buds, so there was good cover.

There! He spotted Dahomey's black mane shining between the silvery branches. The horses were corralled in a shallow ditch surrounded by a fallen branch "fence." Midnight darted toward them. Suddenly a twig broke somewhere to his left. Without thinking, he dropped flat to the ground with a muffled thump. *Now what? Maybe it's just a jackrabbit or some other critter.*

Midnight bobbed up, ready to scramble to his horse.

"*Chk! Chk! Chk!*" He went to his knees again. It was hard trying to make out familiar shapes through the clump of pines growing in the middle of the oaks. Midnight stretched his neck to look harder. Something *did* move. Not an animal, either. He blinked in amazement.

Was it Lou Boy? He scooted on his belly, snakelike, toward a shadow in the trees. When he got to the spot, there was nothing there. He turned back.

"*Chk! Chk!*" The noise was coming from deeper into the trees. *What if there's a soldier out there, trickin' me away so I can't warn the Arapaho that the army's about to move in on the camp? What if they wipe out Winter Mary and the others just like they did at Sand Creek?*

"Midnight! What are you waitin' on? Let's git!" The words were hushed and rushed, but it was definitely Lou Boy! Midnight got to his feet and hurried toward his friend.

"Man, you're alive! You came after me!" Midnight grabbed Lou Boy's shoulders. Lou Boy grabbed

Midnight's arms and looked at him closely, then grinned
and shoved him away.

"Fool. 'Course I came after you! I sure am glad to see
you're still in one piece," he said with relief. He patted
the saddlebag slung across his chest.

"You need anything? Food? Water?" When Midnight
shook his head, Lou Boy went on.

"I yelled at you in the storm and didn't get any answer,
so I doubled back. The snow was so heavy, I couldn't
pick up tracks. I pressed on to get help. The station
wasn't even half an hour away. Joe B. was waiting for
us there. He lent me a little spotted pony in case
Dahomey got lost, too. The snow had stopped by the
time I got into dry duds and found that tree where
you fell and rolled. You broke bushes and branches all
the way down. I managed to pick up the Indians' trail,
but I was already nearly a day's ride behind. I've been
watchin' here for two days, tryin' to figure if you was
dead or alive!"

Midnight shook his head. "Naw, Lou Boy. They never
harmed a hair on me. Dahomey's back yonder. Come
on." Midnight plunged through the trees and bushes
toward the horses, with Lou Boy close behind.

Dahomey saw them coming. He turned his big
brown eyes and shining black head to look at Midnight.
Midnight's eyes brightened. He ran his hands over
Dahomey's shoulders and flanks, then bent to check the
horse's shoes.

"Hey, boy!" Dahomey nuzzled his hair. He was still

saddled. Midnight made a quick check of his saddlebags. Everything was in order. He wasted no more time, mounting Dahomey and starting through the brush.

"Where's Buttercup?"

"Right outside these woods. Midnight! What's got into you?" Lou Boy jogged alongside the horse. He could tell that something had changed.

Midnight took a deep breath. "I know I rushed outta Denver like a barn on fire, ready to go get my folks. Well, I got somethin' to do first."

Lou Boy frowned.

"What're you talking about?" Lou Boy's voice was sharp. "There was a rider just come in to the station before the snow. From the fort. Says the rebs gave up! You hear? Surrendered! The war—it's over!"

Midnight's mouth dropped open. For a minute, he couldn't breathe. His mind went blank. His whole body trembled.

"Midnight? This clears the way for ya, don't it? You got a mission, right? Ain't nothin' to stop you from gettin' your folks outta there now!"

"The North won? It's over?" Midnight's head pounded. Memories of his family burst out of their lonely corners in his mind.

Truth and Queen's laughs ringin' sweet like bells. Mama's hands, sewin' with a needle by candlelight. Papa standin' knee-deep in the creek, holdin' up a fat trout he caught with his bare hands. My big sister, Lady, openin' up her proper starched white kitchen apron and spillin' out flaky biscuits that she snuck from the cookhouse. Mama's voice sayin', "Be strong, my Midnight Son."

The memories were powerful, urging Midnight to ride out of the woods, out of Colorado. Pushing him to head south now and not look back. He gritted his teeth and fought them. In a few minutes he came to himself.

"I'm mighty glad this war is over, Lou Boy. But you know what? That can't change what I'm 'bout to do. If you're with me still, I'll lay it all out for you."

"Let's get on with it, then!" Lou Boy sped through the trees on foot. Midnight rode after him. As the trees thinned and they neared open space, he saw Buttercup. Beside her stood a wiry brown pony with large white patches. Lou Boy mounted his horse silently and they galloped on.

7

The sun was fully up as they rode south. They cut a trail hugging the grassy foothills of the Rockies, staying away from wide-open meadows and any soldiers on patrol around Denver. Lou Boy had the spotted pony trotting behind, tied by a long rope.

"I'm carryin' a message for the Indians," Midnight blurted out. Lou Boy rubbed his chin and kept looking ahead. Midnight continued.

"You don't haveta be part of this. Go on back to the Crazy Eight."

Lou Boy's head spun around.

"You givin' me orders now? Look, I pick my fights—and my friends. I've met every kind of person, Midnight. I know I could trust you with my life if I had to. So whatever you're in for with these Indians, count me with it, okay?"

Midnight had never heard Lou Boy talk with so much feeling.

"Well, it all started with this girl—," he began. Lou Boy let out a loud whistle.

"What?" Midnight stopped.

"Midnight, most every time a cowpoke's story starts with a girl, there's trouble following!"

Any other time, Midnight would've laughed. "If you wanna hear it, Louis Holt, I'll tell ya."

"Oh, he's callin' me by my given name!" Lou Boy glanced at Midnight and saw that he wasn't smiling. "Sorry, Midnight. This ain't no joke, is it?"

"Naw. These Arapahos who picked me up outta that snow, they're trapped against them hills back there and they want me to go for help."

"And bring down a few hundred warriors, huh? Talk at the station was they're lookin' for one Arapaho in particular, sending in reinforcements, too. Must be about six hundred soldiers now. Indian's name was somethin' like Standin' Fox."

Midnight sat up straight. "You mean Big Runnin' Fox, Lou Boy. They got any big guns—cannon?"

"Dunno. But they have rifles."

Midnight shook his head. "Winter Mary and her people don't stand a chance." His voice was caught on the wind. He spurred Dahomey to go faster.

"Midnight, we've been runnin' the horses hard for what, three hours? If we don't let 'em rest—"

"I know, I know."

About half a mile ahead was a clump of bright green pinyon pines stretching out of tall, wild grass. Midnight and Lou Boy stopped at the edge of the forest and turned the horses out to graze. The cowboys sat back to back so one of them could keep watch over the meadow while the other watched the trees. Lou Boy passed his leather water pouch to Midnight.

"You know these cavalry men don't do a thing without orders from the government," Lou Boy said. He pulled a stick of beef jerky from a heavy cloth sack.

"Right. So looks like the U.S. Army is takin' this territory any whichway they can. Indians don't count for nothin' far as they care."

"That ain't the way the story goes in Denver." Lou Boy chewed.

"Looks like most common folks got things wrong 'bout Indians. Same way they got things wrong 'bout people like me." Midnight shook his head and squinted in the sunlight.

Lou Boy pointed out a gray-green mountain ridge far ahead. Each rise was kind of pointed and uneven like the bottom of a bad set of teeth.

"That's north," he told Midnight. "My pa spent time in these parts. So I know we want the Rockies behind us as we head due east. Gotta pass south of Denver and keep on east to hit the Republican River. It's a mighty hard ride, and we're out to make it in a hurry!"

"At least we got the extra horse. Let's do it." Midnight climbed into his saddle and took off. His mind was so set on what he was about to do that he didn't look at the amazing snow-topped mountains standing tall against the sky. And he barely noticed the dark, square shapes of Denver's buildings jutting up from the flat plains sprawling off in the distance.

"Say, Midnight!" Lou Boy whispered, slowing Buttercup and the pony to a walk. "Something moved up ahead! Look!"

Midnight saw it, too. Something dark, for only a second, then it was gone.

"Could've been a scared deer," he said quietly, keeping his eyes on the grass. "Also could be bandits ready to jump us. Let's check it out."

Midnight scrambled out of his saddle and crouched low in the grass. Lou Boy was beside him.

They inched forward. Midnight tilted his head, motioning for Lou Boy to circle around to the other side. Midnight dropped Dahomey's reins, steadying him with a slow stroke against his jaw.

Suddenly the grass stopped moving. Midnight stopped, too. His eyes met Lou Boy's. Then they heard it. A human sound. A hurting sound.

Midnight stomped through the grass and almost tripped over the Indian crouched near the ground. A sweaty, dirt-streaked face turned up to look at them.

"Eagle Eye!" Midnight gasped.

"D-Dark One!" Eagle Eye blinked at him. He held his left arm close to his body as if he were hurt, but Midnight couldn't see any blood.

"He's from the camp, Lou Boy. Pass the water." Lou Boy came forward.

Eagle Eye trickled the water over his cracking lips. He struggled to his knees.

"I have only a flesh wound." Midnight helped him stand.

"Who did this to you?" Midnight's heart began to beat fast. He knew without hearing it. Soldiers!

Eagle Eye grabbed Midnight's shirt in one fist, pulling him close. He was searching Midnight's eyes, looking for something. Midnight stared into his, but they weren't angry as he expected. They were scared. Eagle Eye held Midnight tight, so close that his shallow breaths were hot against Midnight's cheek.

"I must get back to warn my people." Eagle Eye spat the words out hoarsely.

"We'll go!" Midnight said. "Let's get you on a horse."

"NO!" he shouted. "The bluecoats thought I was dead. I heard them say my father had been found! I *must* warn him. Give me a horse and I will go alone!" He was looking wildly from Midnight to Lou Boy.

Midnight knew that he'd already made a big mistake in not taking the Arapahos' message right away. He wasn't going to make another one. There was no way he'd let Eagle Eye go back by himself.

"You wanted my help, didn't you? Now you got it. Come on, Lou Boy."

Eagle Eye walked stiffly over to the pony. He seemed to have trouble climbing up. Midnight gave him a boost. Eagle Eye's thanks was an angry grunt. Eagle Eye didn't wait—he took off as soon as Midnight let him go. Midnight and Lou Boy got back in their saddles.

"Dahomey," Midnight said in a whisper, "you go like the wind. For me, and for Winter Mary!"

★　★　★

They flew across the plains. The sun had rolled over them and now hung low over the Rockies. Eagle Eye was leaning heavily against his horse. Midnight thought he might be more injured than he said. Yet somehow Eagle Eye willed himself to grip the pony's mane and hang on. Midnight dug his heels into Dahomey's flanks, pushing him to gallop even harder.

First they saw the buzzards swooping in and out of the jagged red hills at the edge of the cottonwoods. Lou Boy looked over at Midnight in silence. Midnight swallowed hard. Then he saw faint wisps of smoke curling up above the trees like beckoning fingers.

Dahomey tore between the trees like he was being chased. Lou Boy and Buttercup were on his tail. They got closer to the camp. Smoke filled their noses and throats. Midnight's eyes were stinging, partly from the air and partly from sudden tears that tried to push themselves out. He brushed away the tears with his sleeve, but he couldn't get rid of the fear.

Eagle Eye threw himself off the pony's back, falling and rising to his feet. Midnight jumped down, catching Eagle Eye's arm to hold him up. Lou Boy quickly tied the horses to one of the thin trees. The three stumbled to the clearing.

"No!" Eagle Eye wailed in a raw voice that carried through the woods and beyond. All the tipis, the lean-tos—everything—had been burned to the ground. Midnight's legs went wobbly, but he knew he had to stand or they would all fall.

Eagle Eye pushed them away and staggered a few paces. Heaps of blackened branches and ashes smoldered where Big Running Fox's tipi once stood. Eagle Eye dropped to his knees.

Midnight remembered the first time—*was it only yesterday?*—that he'd walked through the camp. The quiet had made him uneasy. So many people, no noise. Now a strange, sad feeling moved around his body, pulling his feet forward onto the burned grass.

I've seen some bad stuff in my fifteen years. Cows piled up on the trail, stiff and dead from drinkin' poison water . . . mad dogs, crazy with rabies, foamin' at the mouth and eatin' at their own tails . . . men and women beaten bloody for tryin' to learn letters or snatchin' a pail of milk for their babies. All them things put together don't add up to this!

Eagle Eye was plodding one heavy foot at a time right ahead of Midnight and Lou Boy. Midnight wanted to say something, but what? No words seemed right.

They saw no one. The air was still warm. Red-orange

embers glowed here and there. Midnight raised his eyes up from that terrible ground.

Between two rocks he could see Winter Mary's clear moon eyes. There she was, half sitting and half kneeling, with Raven Woman lying in her arms.

8

"**She said you would** come back," Winter Mary said in a small voice. Now she sounded more like a little girl than the high-spirited young woman Midnight had seen before. Eagle Eye laid a hand on Midnight's shoulder to steady himself. Then with a straight back and square shoulders, he walked closer to the women.

Eagle Eye knelt slowly. Raven Woman's eyes fluttered open, but she didn't move.

"They came for our father with cannons!" Winter Mary's voice rose angrily. Her eyes flashed at her brother.

"Many of us were already scattered in the woods with our bundles when the earth began to shake. The cannon shots were like thunder around us. Bluecoats were everywhere. Our people ran in many directions. So much confusion! Father had just stepped from his tent to speak to a brave."

She took a deep breath of the smoky air and began to cough.

"And then?" Eagle Eye sounded perfectly calm, but Midnight could imagine the feelings twisting inside him. Winter Mary pressed one hand to her chest and began again. This time the anger was gone.

"Ne'ina pulled me back. They fired—Father fell into the tent. They fired again. Ne'ina threw me to the ground and fell on top of me. 'Don't move!' she said. I closed my eyes. I heard more shooting, screaming. I acted as if I was . . . dead." Winter Mary jerked her head toward the woods with wide eyes as if it was happening over again. Midnight peeled off his jacket and threw it awkwardly around her trembling shoulders.

Midnight spoke in a harsh whisper to Lou Boy. "I was a fool. Maybe even a coward. Big Runnin' Fox, their pa, tried to make me see. If I'd made the right choice and left here yesterday instead of Eagle Eye, I could've passed that patrol without bein' stopped!"

"But Midnight—"

"Just leave me be!" Midnight pushed his fists deep inside his pants pockets and traced a circle in the dirt with his boot tip.

"Midnight Son." Raven Woman's voice called to him weakly. Midnight sighed deeply and turned around. Winter Mary was gently stroking her mother's hair. Eagle Eye sat beside them with his head bowed low. Raven Woman stretched her fingers out to Midnight.

He squatted down to take them. Her hand was so warm. Midnight was too ashamed to look at her. His eyes flitted around. He saw hands ... Winter Mary's, small and plump, Eagle Eye's, big and long fingered. Lou Boy's, sunburned. Midnight's own rough, coffee hands.

"Look to me, boy child." Raven Woman didn't ask; she commanded. Midnight obeyed. She was dying, and they all knew it.

"Clear your mind, boy child. Don't keep this thing heavy on yourself. You came back, you see. A dream is a powerful thing, ain't it? Dream made you choose one way and to follow that. For your family. Then a dream made you change your mind, yes?" All Midnight could do was nod.

Raven Woman smiled and squeezed Midnight's hand.

"I had dreams, too, Midnight. Way long time ago. Dreams told me you was comin'. I been waitin' on you. Listen to me." She stopped, taking a breath.

"Just like you can't never give up on seein' your people again, I never could. My two"—she rolled her head to look from Winter Mary to Eagle Eye—"were born and raised Arapaho. Now I want them to know *my* people. You take them east, Midnight Son. You put my girl's hand in my sister's hand."

Midnight's mouth dropped open.

"This is my wish. Once you find your family, do this for Raven Woman."

Midnight looked quickly at Eagle Eye. He kept

his head down. Winter Mary stared straight at him. Midnight blinked and made himself look into Raven Woman's eyes.

"I—I will, Raven Woman."

She closed her eyes. "I knew I . . . was right . . . about you. . . ." Her voice trailed off softly. Her fingers began to slip from his. He squeezed them more tightly.

"My . . . children . . ." Raven Woman's words were no more than a breath. The words blew away with a cool wind that came up suddenly around them. Midnight felt the wind on his face. A tingling sensation rippled down through his entire body. Winter Mary jerked her head up. Eagle Eye trembled. Lou Boy rubbed at his arms and stomped his feet as if they'd gone to sleep.

"She is dead," Eagle Eye said simply. "Now she will be free forever."

"Ne'ina," Winter Mary whispered gently.

Midnight released Raven Woman's hand. His sadness went deep, as if Raven Woman was his own mother. Winter Mary dropped her eyes, fingering the edges of her mother's silver belt. Silent tears rolled down her dusty cheeks.

"Lou Boy and me—we'll leave you for a while." Midnight looked away quickly. Watching was too painful.

No use sayin' that I believe Raven Woman sent that wind to blow us together, let us know that she means for us to carry out her plan. But will Eagle Eye go along with it? What she

*said about trust—that it's a funny thing—is sure right. And
I don't believe Eagle Eye trusts me one bit.*

★   ★   ★

Night fell, and hours later they buried Raven Woman
on a rocky hill under a bright full moon. Winter Mary's
dark, kneeling figure made a shadow picture against the
white rocks. Eagle Eye had remained huddled near the
grave, his face closed against the world.

Midnight and Lou Boy had searched for Big Running
Fox's body but found nothing. They guessed he had
been burned with his tipi. In the daylight they had seen
bloodstains on some leaves, signs that others had been
wounded. But now they found only scattered bundles
and packages. It seemed as if the other Arapaho had simply vanished. Midnight guessed that once the soldiers
had brought Big Running Fox down, there was no need
to hang around such a small camp. They'd probably left it
to burn and marched their terrified prisoners to the fort.
At least, he hoped so.

After their search, Lou Boy cleared a spot to make a
small fire. He had a little coffee in his saddlebag, and the
night was chilly. Midnight felt funny about doing that,
especially after what had happened. So they agreed to
keep it as far away from the camp as possible.

When Winter Mary walked over, they were startled.
Her hair hung loose and wild—half the length it had
been. Her tunic was covered with red dirt, and a sleeve
had been torn off. Midnight jumped up.

"Please. I am not hurt." She shifted a sooty bundle from one arm to the other. "Arapaho do this to show our sorrow." She set the bundle carefully on the ground and opened it. There were things she'd collected from the woods: a charred metal pot, a wooden spoon, a smoky-smelling buffalo robe, some rolled clothing, and an old Bible.

Midnight watched her open the yellowed pages fondly, as if she had done this many times before.

"You can read?" Midnight sat beside her and looked at the scratchy marks written inside the front of the book.

"Ne'ina taught me. She learned in secret from the child she cared for. This"—Winter Mary pointed to the handwriting—"is the family name of those who kept her as a slave." She closed the book. The anger came back to her words.

"What kind of people are these, Midnight Son? They are stealing the land of our people from under our feet! They stole your life, my mother's and father's too! Can we never win the fight against them?"

Midnight stared into the campfire. How many times had he wondered the same? Midnight looked at Winter Mary. She was waiting for his answer.

"Look at us. We're still standin', ain't we? Seems like part of this game is to keep on standin' when somebody wants to knock you flat down. I don't plan on losin', Winter Mary. I'm gonna live the best life I can, no matter what!"

Lou Boy rattled the tin pot as he made the coffee.

"He's a hardheaded fella, Winter Mary, but listen to him," Lou Boy said. "Look at us here. By all rights and laws of some folks, Midnight and me oughta hate each other's guts. But we know each other for real. So we don't pay that stuff no mind."

Winter Mary looked from one of them to the other as if she were trying to see how deep their friendship really was.

"It will not be easy for us to go on," she said.

Midnight shook his head. "Was it ever easy?"

Lou Boy interrupted. "When did you last eat?" he asked, holding out some beef jerky.

She shook her head to refuse. "It is not the Arapaho way. When someone dies, we do not eat. We do not braid our hair. We sit at the burial place to do our crying." She looked away from them toward the hills.

Midnight sighed. "So you think your brother's gonna sit up on that hill all night?"

"He is grieving. I must go there, too. Arapaho sometimes sit at the burial place for days. Eagle Eye is thinking as I do: Where will we go now? Our ancestors are buried here. Now our parents. When we leave this land, we leave everything. We are the last of our clan."

"I'm the last of my clan, too," Lou Boy said quietly. "Ma and Pa are both gone. Never had no brothers or sisters. Sometimes I think it oughta be easy to live on my own with nobody to answer to, nobody to worry about. But bein' alone ain't no picnic. Guess that's why Midnight and me stick together, huh?"

Winter Mary said nothing. Midnight hunched his shoulders. Her silence was awful.

"Winter Mary," he started, hoping that she would shift her look to him instead of the fire.

"That war the bluecoats been fightin' out east is over. Nothin' will keep them from floodin' this territory with soldiers now. Your pa wasn't safe before, and you sure ain't safe here now. You gotta leave Colorado. Question is, will Eagle Eye go?"

"My mother wished it," she declared firmly.

Lou Boy clinked a tin coffee cup against a rock. "Yeah, but—"

"AHHHH!" Eagle Eye's wail sliced through their conversation. Winter Mary darted off like a doe heading for the sound of her fawn in trouble. Midnight and Lou Boy leapt to their feet, cups and coffee flying.

"Nothing must happen to him! He is all I have left!" she panted. Midnight and Lou Boy followed at her heels.

"You got us, for whatever we're worth!" Midnight shouted out.

"AAAAHHHHHHHH!" Midnight winced at the sound. Against the quiet of the night, it was the scariest sound he had ever heard. He and Lou Boy were fast on their feet, but Winter Mary was faster. She was already at her brother's side before they cleared the edge of the woods.

Eagle Eye was staggering wildly through the ashes, his long black hair streaming loose around his tearful face.

His chest heaved as he yelled his pain and sorrow into the darkness.

"Eagle Eye." Midnight moved slowly and spoke calmly. "Look at me." Midnight was close enough to touch his arm. "I know your heart hurts bad."

"Brother!" Winter Mary called out. Eagle Eye moved toward her and his torn shirt dropped open. There, just above three small blue circles tattooed across his chest, was an ugly purple tear in his skin, oozing blood. Midnight gasped.

"He is shot!" she cried out.

"We never knew it was a gunshot wound!" Midnight told her.

Eagle Eye slumped against Midnight, giving in to his pain at last.

"We . . . were too late," he muttered hoarsely. Then he collapsed.

Winter Mary dropped to his side and put her hand across his brow.

"He is burning with fever," she said, frowning.

Midnight lifted the edge of Eagle Eye's tunic. "The bullet's deep. It's gotta come out, or he won't have a chance of makin' it."

Winter Mary looked alarmed. "I can't—"

Midnight swallowed hard. She had been through enough already.

"I ain't never done this before. I gotta be honest."

"Do it," Winter Mary said forcefully.

"Let's get him to the fire." Midnight lifted his shoulders. Lou Boy took Eagle Eye's feet. Winter Mary plunged ahead, squinting in the moonlight to pick up more things from the ground as she went. By the time they got Eagle Eye to the fireside, she had spread out a buffalo skin for him to lie on.

Midnight squatted and looked carefully at the spot high on Eagle Eye's chest.

"I'll need somethin' to cut with." Lou Boy flashed the blade of the small bone-handled knife that he always carried in his boot.

"What else?" Winter Mary showed them two full water pouches and a roll of slightly burned cloth. "These were dropped in the woods."

Midnight nodded and pushed up his sleeves. He snatched up a stick.

"Lou Boy, put this between Eagle Eye's teeth. Winter Mary, clean his wound as good as you can." Midnight dripped water over his fingers, then took up the knife. He thrust it into the campfire to burn it clean.

"We have him down tight, Midnight," Lou Boy said.

Midnight pursed his lips and turned around. He laid one hand gently on Eagle Eye's chest. He could feel Eagle Eye's heart and his own, pounding the same wild beat.

Steady, Midnight told himself.

He touched the red-hot tip of the knife against the skin for a second, then pushed it down into the hole carefully. Blood rose up around the metal.

"Grrr . . . GRRR!" Eagle Eye growled around the stick, his body shuddering. Winter Mary pressed him down.

"Quickly!" she urged. Midnight moved the knife deeper to search for the bullet.

"AHHH!" Eagle Eye spat the stick out. Midnight swung his head to one side. The knife flew into the air.

"Eagle Eye! Do not move!" Winter Mary shouted. Midnight grabbed the knife up and stuck it into the flames again. Moving fast, he eased it in again. Eagle Eye moaned and lay still.

"Here!" Midnight popped the bloody silver shape out, holding it in the air. Lou Boy ripped the cloth into strips, passing them to Winter Mary. Midnight helped her wrap the bandage tightly around Eagle Eye's chest and shoulder.

"It's out." Midnight sat back, hardly able to believe what he had done.

"Thank you, Midnight Son." Winter Mary said it plain, no pretty words or long speeches. Midnight was too weary to answer with anything more than a smile.

9

When the sun came up, it brought crisp spring air and sharp, clear skies. Midnight blinked awake and realized that he hadn't dreamed at all. No nightmares, nothing. Maybe yesterday had drained everything out of him. Now he just felt tired. He stretched slowly and sat up.

Lou Boy and Winter Mary were gone. Midnight figured that Lou Boy was scouting the trail ahead. The small fire from last night had died, so Winter Mary might have set out looking for fresh kindling. Eagle Eye lay next to him wrapped in the buffalo robe. If anybody had truly been drained—of blood as well as feeling—it was him.

There was a sound behind them. Midnight jumped up. Winter Mary walked out of the trees, carrying quail eggs.

"You rattled me!" Midnight's muscles were still tight and tense.

"I am sorry. I went early to sit on the hill. Then I got these eggs to cook for Eagle Eye." Midnight relaxed a little. He noticed that Winter Mary's chin was scratched. He'd never even thought that she might have been hurt, too.

"Winter Mary, I—" He wanted to stop, to choose his words. But he forced himself to get on with it.

"For the rest of my natural life, I will carry the shame of causin' this." He gulped. "This awful *thing* to happen to your people, your folks, to Eagle Eye. I—" He couldn't go on or look at her.

Winter Mary's round hand touched his. For one moment, their two hands reminded him of branches on a tree. Different coloring, different sizes, but connected. He thought she would pull her hand away instantly, but she didn't.

She sighed. "You did not fire the cannon. And you saved Eagle Eye's life! You carry no shame, Midnight."

"Still, I won't never forgive myself."

"Never is a long time." Eagle Eye suddenly broke in. Both Midnight and Winter Mary turned to him at once.

Winter Mary gently eased her hand from Midnight's, then went to busy herself with the eggs and the fire.

Eagle Eye was trying to sit up. Midnight leaned over to offer his arm. Eagle Eye looked at him hard, squinting. Then he grabbed Midnight's upper arm and pulled himself to sitting. Midnight shoved his own rolled blanket against the small of Eagle Eye's back.

Eagle Eye settled himself. He touched the bandage, tilting his head to one side.

"You tended my wound," he said.

"I took out that bullet, yeah."

"Mmm" was all Eagle Eye said. He shut his eyes tight for a second, as if he were trying to push the pain away.

"You two really wanna go through with this, follow Raven Woman's word and leave your land?" Midnight asked.

"We love the land. She loved her people more. But my mother was not Arapaho," Eagle Eye replied.

Winter Mary spoke quietly from the fire. "No, she was not." She stirred the sizzling pan furiously.

Eagle Eye had no energy to argue. He winced and lay down again. Midnight went to kneel at the fire.

"I know you don't wanna leave your mama and papa here, Winter Mary. But—"

"We cannot leave." She wiped her sleeve across her eyes. "Not yet. Please let me sit with them three or four more sleeps. I don't know when I will come to this place again!"

Midnight didn't have the heart to remind her of the dangers. With nothing else to say, he arose and walked slowly away from the trail, looking for Lou Boy. They would just have to wait.

★   ★   ★

A few days later Lou Boy came crashing through the bushes, hair flying and eyes wide. Midnight and Winter Mary both sprang protectively to Eagle Eye.

"We gotta get a move on now, folks," Lou Boy panted. "I spotted riders combing the hills. Looks like they got Indians with them!"

"How can that be?" Midnight looked at Winter Mary. "Prisoners?"

Eagle Eye moved. "Pawnee!" he breathed.

"The Pawnee nation is enemy to the Arapaho," Winter Mary told them. "Pawnee fight with bluecoats against us. If they are searching, they are looking for Eagle Eye."

Eagle Eye pulled himself up. "The Pawnee will think I have gone to bring warriors against the bluecoats. We are in great danger! We must go north to the Republican River!"

"I will fill the water pouches at the stream." Winter Mary moved like a whirlwind.

"Wait!" Midnight held Eagle Eye down. "When we leave here, we're goin' south. If we're doin' what Raven Woman wanted, your battle with the bluecoats ends here!"

Eagle Eye ignored him. "I must go back to our camp once more. There are things I need."

Midnight was just as strong willed as he was. "Listen to me! I'm the one who promised your mama I'd get y'all to Missouri. But I'm goin' back to Texas first. We need a plan, and I'm gonna have my say. Anybody wanna wrangle me over that?"

None of the others made a sound. Midnight took that as agreement. He dropped to his knees and picked up a twig. He rubbed the ground smooth and started drawing a line.

"I figure now we can skip around Fort Lyon and follow the Santa Fe overland trail into Kansas, to Fort Dodge. From there we pick up the trail into Texas. The Greely plantation where my folks are is south, toward Austin. Fort Dodge is a week's ride, give or take a day. Winter Mary, you think you can scrounge any food from your camp to help get us there?"

"Water is plentiful, but not much else. We must hunt along the way."

Lou Boy cleared his throat. "Whatever else we need will have to wait till Fort Dodge, then."

Eagle Eye looked from Lou Boy to Midnight. "And do you expect two Arapaho to ride into the gates with you there?" Midnight shot him a nasty look.

" 'Course not. Lou Boy and me can handle it. Let's just get there."

"Let us stop wasting time," Winter Mary declared. "We will gather up our things." She set off toward the remains of the camp. Lou Boy saw Midnight follow her with his eyes.

"Remember," Lou Boy whispered under his breath to Midnight. "It all started with a girl."

Eagle Eye hissed, "Not the Arapaho one!" He made it to his feet and slowly followed his sister.

Midnight refused to answer or look at either of them. *What are they talkin' about, anyway? I ain't got time to get*

*soft on no girl. I got miles to go before I can lay my heart
down. When I do, it's gonna be at my mama's feet.*

Midnight headed for Dahomey. The horses needed
to graze and be watered before they set off. He unhitched
all three and led them out of the woods to the flat
grassland.

When he looked across the plains and saw the sun
creeping up the edge of the sky, he thought of the days
when he'd been on the run. Papa had told him to ride
by night and hide by day. He had spent many hours
crouched in the branches of trees, afraid to move or
breathe. Midnight shaded his eyes with one hand and
looked directly up at the glowing ball of light.

"You ain't got sunstruck, have ya?" Lou Boy walked up
behind him. He strolled over to Buttercup and scratched
between her ears. Midnight lowered his hand and shook
his head.

"Naw. Just thinkin', that's all. It's funny, I thought that
once I made it to freedom, once I was my own man, the
world would stop or somethin'. But I'm findin' out that
freedom has got its own rules."

"Yeah? Like what?"

"Like a free man has still gotta turn around and lend a
hand to somebody else climbin' the same mountain.
'Cause a free man don't ever know when his own foot's
gonna slip!"

"You're right about that, partner. Now think on something else. Eagle Eye's not too keen on followin' us across

the country. Any way you look at it, travelin' through Colorado Territory with an Indian brave is like travelin' with a man with a bounty on his head."

"Somethin' like travelin' with an escaped slave, huh?" Midnight looked sideways at Lou Boy.

"Aw, now . . . you know I didn't mean nothin' like that!"

"I guess, Lou Boy. It's hard to know what anything really means these days, ain't it? Let's just get goin'." Midnight mounted Dahomey who gently nudged the spotted pony.

"This horse got a name?" Midnight asked, trotting back to the edge of the woods.

"Whatever we like. Joe B. got him thrown in with the deal at the fort."

"Maybe Winter Mary and Eagle Eye can keep the horse. I'll settle with Joe B. when this is all said and done. Say, Lou Boy—" Midnight stopped. "Did you say anything to Joe B. about what I told ya? Me goin' for my folks?"

Lou Boy answered easily. "Sure did. You never said it was a secret. I told him we'd keep in touch. He says we can work for him anytime."

Eagle Eye stepped out of the woods slowly, but on his own. Slung over his right shoulder was a bow and deerskin quiver filled with feather-tailed arrows.

Winter Mary popped out of the trees behind him with water pouches and rolled bundles under each arm. She had pulled her short braids up with Raven Woman's hairpin. Midnight also noticed that the same hammered silver belt that Raven Woman had worn was hanging around Winter Mary's waist now. A small bow made of buffalo horn and her quiver were looped over one shoulder. Midnight was surprised.

Winter Mary looked straight past him to the spotted pony. She strode toward the horses, once again moving much more quickly than it seemed her short legs could truly carry her. She stroked the pony's nose, making small sounds into his ears.

"What is he called?" she asked Midnight as she walked around him.

"Ain't got no name."

"His spots are like clouds in the sky," she said. "I will call him Cloud."

In minutes Winter Mary had Cloud loaded. She helped her brother on, then climbed up behind him.

"All set?" Midnight breathed deeply. They turned the horses and rode off side by side.

"Not lookin' back?" Lou Boy called to Eagle Eye. His hair rippled out behind him like a horse's mane. Eagle Eye's jaw was set hard as stone. He didn't answer, but his sister did.

Winter Mary's words flew back to him over the moving air. "Not when I know that we will return!"

10

There was no place to hide on the plains. They could have taken the careful way as Midnight and Lou Boy had before, riding in the shadows of the Southern Rockies. But they wanted fast travel, both to outrun the soldiers and to find a safe place for Eagle Eye to rest. They drove the horses from sunup to sundown, with Lou Boy and Midnight taking turns scouting ahead.

Midnight tried to coax Winter Mary to talk, but she was too concerned about her brother to pay much attention. The rough riding was only making him weaker. He hung in and hung on at first, but after four days of travel, the fever came back strong.

"Midnight!" Winter Mary pulled Cloud up alongside Dahomey. Midnight could see the sweat on Eagle Eye's cheek as he slumped toward Cloud's back. He could hear Eagle Eye's shallow breaths.

"My brother cannot go on. He needs to be still so the bleeding will stop."

"Right. Let's make camp over there." Midnight pointed to a couple of scrawny shade trees. "They're close to the trail. Lou Boy will find us easy. Lemme help you get him down."

Midnight could feel the fever's heat as he touched Eagle Eye. Winter Mary unrolled the buffalo skin onto the ground, making a soft pallet. They eased Eagle Eye from Cloud's back and half-carried, half-dragged him to it.

Winter Mary poured water onto a scrap of cloth. Midnight squatted beside them. Eagle Eye's bandage had a growing red stain.

"We need clean bandage. More water. Time." She wiped Eagle Eye's face.

"I ain't leavin' you alone here. Fort Lyon is half a day away. When Lou Boy comes back, one of us can go for bandages and water. But time—the longer we stay, the more likely some patrol is to catch us here." Midnight stood up.

He sighted a distant rider coming over one of the hills.

"Somebody's comin'!" he said. "Quick! Cover Eagle Eye with my blanket."

Midnight planted his feet and stood firmly. He curled his fingers around the smooth palm-sized throwing stone hidden in his waistcoat pocket. He had never been able to abide guns or whips, not after seeing them turned on slaves so often. A good stone was the only weapon he'd ever carried as a free man, and he had a deadly aim. Winter Mary, however, readied her bow.

"You really good with that thing?" Midnight asked without turning his head.

"You will find out how good I am!"

"Hope not," Midnight mumbled.

The rider waved a hand in the air and Midnight knew instantly who it was. His shoulders relaxed.

"Lou Boy." Winter Mary slipped the arrow back into the quiver.

"All clear ahead! I rode three or four miles, didn't see one bluecoat." Lou Boy slapped his dusty hat against his leg. "He sleeping?"

"Yes," Winter Mary answered.

Midnight snapped his fingers. "My mama knew how to make this tea from wild sage leaves for chills and fever. I'll see if I can find some sage around here."

"I will try anything." Winter Mary seemed wanting to be busy.

So they agreed. Lou Boy stayed with Eagle Eye while Midnight and Winter Mary went looking for wild sage. Midnight had seen what looked like creek water about a half mile back. They went for it, fanning out over a wide area with heads bent.

"It's a short bush," Midnight explained, "with a clump of lil' purple flowers 'bout the size of your fist."

The prairie grass began to slope downward a bit and Midnight saw the creek. It sure would be nice to have fish for supper. After everything they'd been through, the sweet, smoky flavor of trout cooked over the fire would be a welcome change.

"Look! Is this it?" Winter Mary plucked up a bunch of full purple blossoms.

"Yes, ma'am!" Midnight helped her fill a pouch with finger-length leaves. Then she watched as he rolled up his pants and waded into the knee-deep water. He stood motionless, just like his papa had taught him. His eyes followed the silvery forms of the fish as they wriggled around and through his legs.

"Plop!" Midnight's hand shot in and out of the water, coming up with a flopping fish. He tossed it onto the bank. Winter Mary smiled! Midnight caught three more and sloshed out of the water.

"You are a good fisherman." Winter Mary opened an extra pouch for the fish.

"Thanks." They trudged up the slope to make their way back.

"Tell me, Midnight Son, about your sisters."

"My sisters?"

"My mother still had much feeling for her sister. What are yours like?"

It was a question he hadn't expected. Once he started talking, though, he found that he was happy at the chance.

"Well . . . I got three. There's Truth. She's nigh ten years old now. Tall, like me. Quiet like, always watchin' folks. She's slow to smile and when she does, it's kinda wide and one-sided. On the plantation she worked in the house cleanin' and learnin' some needlework. I believe she likes that, always bringin' some scrap to show Mama what she did. And Queen. The baby. She's built round and she's fast, like you. Talk about a hot temper! Only knee-high to a grasshopper, but they couldn't make her do nothin' she didn't want to. She broke up dishes and spilled pots till master's wife sent her outside to work the garden. That Queen likes it in the wide open." Midnight smiled broadly, remembering.

"And the other one?" Winter Mary kept up with his long-legged steps.

"Lady. She got sold off long time before Truth and Queen was born. She was sweet as candy to me. Always wantin' to give me stuff, and we never had nothin'. So it was a little round pebble or a hot biscuit she swiped outta that kitchen. We used to whisper together when we were supposed to be sleepin'!"

Midnight suddenly looked up at the sky as if he expected to see Lady there. "Not a day goes by that I don't wonder where she is."

"Arapaho brothers and sisters do not whisper together," Winter Mary said, squinting to see how close their campsite was. "Eagle Eye will always protect me. But . . . it would be very different to have a brother like you."

"Good different or bad different?" Midnight asked playfully.

Winter Mary considered carefully before she answered him.

"I will let you know at the end of the journey." She picked up the walking pace, and before Midnight knew it, she was way in front of him.

"Hey!" Midnight said in a voice so low that she couldn't possibly hear. "That's somethin' to look forward to."

★　★　★

The sage tea and solid ground did wonders for Eagle Eye. He slept for the rest of the afternoon and through the night, with his sister at his side.

"Mornin', Winter Mary," Midnight said. "Any change?"

"He is good. More rest and clean bandages will help."

Lou Boy sat up. "I'll ride to the fort. Be back by sundown. I can get supplies. Buttercup and I'll travel as fast as we can!"

Lou Boy gulped coffee and galloped away. Midnight wandered over to Dahomey and ran his fingers through the horse's mane. It was tangled. Midnight opened his saddlebag and pulled out a sturdy brush. He unbuckled the saddle girth and carefully lifted the saddle off. Very slowly he passed the brush across Dahomey's shining black flanks. Down and up again. Covering one side, then moving around to the other. He pulled the brush through Dahomey's thick mane and tail, catching bits of leaves and easing away the knots.

He stepped back to look at his work. Dahomey shook his mane out, then walked off and set to serious nibbling of the sweet grass at his feet. Midnight followed into the meadow behind him. He'd known so little about horses before Mexico, before Dahomey. Then Papa had shoved those reins into his hands, and this fine beast carried him right out of bondage. Midnight reached down to pluck a blade of the grass. He rolled it between his fingers and watched Dahomey with pride.

11

Midnight finally got to his feet, stretching his legs and shaking them out. He turned to stroll back, picking up the brush as he went. Winter Mary was sitting with the Bible book on her lap.

"Y'know, I've learned to rope cattle and brand 'em, and even make decent coffee, but I sure envy a body who knows letters!"

"Come here, Midnight Son." Winter Mary closed the book and reached to pull a pencil-sized twig from the ash near the dying campfire. Midnight knelt to see what she was about to do.

"See this." She began to draw in the dry dirt with the twig, speaking as she made each form.

"*M*." She scraped up, down, up, down. "*I-D-N-I-G-H-T.* Can you do it the same?"

Midnight chuckled and played the game, using his

pointer finger to make crooked copies of Winter Mary's work. Finished, he grinned at her.

"This is your name," she said in a quiet voice that echoed in Midnight's head. His grin fell open. He touched the letters with his fingertips.

"Midnight? This is what I look like in letters? You sayin' I just wrote my own *name*?"

"You did!" For the first time since the massacre, the light was back on in Winter Mary's eyes.

She went on to read out loud and Midnight listened, as much to Winter Mary's clear, even voice as to the words she was speaking.

Time passed them by. The sun began to sink behind distant hills. The sound of hooves slapping on the ground caught both of them by surprise. Lou Boy rode up, breathless.

"Took my time gettin' there, but I hurried back. Got some things from the fort store." He unfurled a brown paper package. Winter Mary rushed to catch the contents.

"The bandage!"

"Yeah, and quinine to help keep that fever down."

Midnight checked the ring of rocks around the ashes. "I'll rebuild this fire so you can have hot water." He quickly added some dry brush and twigs. He struck a small stone with a knife to light a spark. Winter Mary put water into the battered pot to boil and set to work with the bandages.

"Psst!" Lou Boy stepped close to Midnight.

"What is it?" Midnight tore open the crackers Lou Boy had bought.

"The next patrol from Fort Lyon is headin' up north. They're thinkin' just like Eagle Eye said—that a bunch of Arapaho will strike back from the Republican River. And somethin' else—" He lowered his voice more.

"I heard that Fort Dodge is just waitin' for the go-ahead to attack the Indians around there. Arapaho, Comanche, Cheyenne. We gotta go straight through, Midnight! And one more thing. The fella in the store tried to make a fuss, specially when I asked for the quinine. I told him that you were the one who was hurt. I don't think he bought the story. The guard looked at me kinda sideways as I left."

"You sayin' they might send somebody to check it out? They got manpower to waste on us?"

"I'm saying they might start to wondering why I didn't bring you in to a doctor. We gotta move along!"

Winter Mary wiped her hands on her tunic and walked over to the boys. "Did you hear any word of our people?"

Lou Boy clutched the brim of his hat. "I—I don't know the particulars. Nobody made it to the fort."

Winter Mary looked back at her brother.

Lou Boy added, "I'm afraid they might send a patrol this way."

Midnight touched Winter Mary's shoulder. "You all right? This is rough news."

Winter Mary turned away. "It is better to know."

Lou Boy knelt over a rough map he was drawing in the dirt. "Listen. I happen to know the country around Fort Dodge."

"You know how we can get outta here?" Midnight asked.

"Here's the Kansas border. We're a day's ride away." Lou Boy pointed to the ground. "See, this is the Arkansas River and Fort Dodge."

Winter Mary stood over them, studying the map. "There was a camp of Arapaho near this Arkansas River," she said, not realizing that Midnight and Lou Boy already knew. "My father spoke of it. If bluecoats follow us—"

"We could lead them straight to our people!" Eagle Eye leaned on one elbow.

"How come you always makin' like you're out of it, then you jumpin' in all over us?" Midnight snapped.

"The son of a Fox has big ears." Eagle Eye threw the blanket off and ran his eyes over the land, bringing them to rest angrily on his sister.

"How far are we from the Republican River? Why didn't you make them go north?" he thundered.

"Because I want to go south. Because Ne'ina wanted this." Winter Mary didn't back down.

"You have no right to decide!" Eagle Eye fumed as he rose shakily to his feet.

"Whoa!" Midnight quickly stood up. "Hold on. I can't let you speak to Winter Mary like that—or dishonor Raven Woman! You do as you please, Eagle Eye—stay with us or go. Winter Mary's got a right to decide for herself!" Lou Boy stepped between them.

"Enough!" Winter Mary threw her hands into the air. "I *have* decided, so you vultures may stop your fight."

Eagle Eye met Midnight's glare head-on over Lou Boy's arm. Midnight wasn't going to hit a wounded man, but he was ready for anything Eagle Eye might do. Yet looking into Eagle Eye's face, he saw pride. And he saw anger there and sadness. Midnight held back.

"I am not a fool," Eagle Eye said. He touched his bandage. "With this, I—we—could not have traveled alone."

"You mean to say you *need* us?" Midnight asked.

Eagle Eye sighed a little. "I said what I meant. My mother was one of your people. She is a great part of me. I want to follow her wishes, if only for my sister's sake. But I am Arapaho inside my bones. I know I cannot easily live in a world that is not Arapaho."

Midnight touched Eagle Eye's arm. "I know better than you think I do 'bout different worlds. So are you with us on this trip to Texas?"

"We are." Eagle Eye spoke up this time. Winter Mary folded her arms across her chest.

"Good." Midnight nodded. "Now much as I hate to say it—it looks like we oughta split up. Be harder for soldiers to follow two trails. We'll meet somewhere in Kansas."

"This is what Arapaho warriors would do!" Eagle Eye made his way to their map and eased to the ground to view it.

"I know this hunting land. I will make another plan for you. Bluecoats will expect Indians to ride the pony." He pointed to Cloud's hooves. "No covering on the foot of an Indian horse."

Lou Boy whistled. "Right! No horseshoes. Joe B. bought this pony fresh broken. So we switch horses!"

Midnight was excited. They all were. "Lou Boy told 'em I was busted up by Indians. Makes sense that they'd think we got our hands on an Indian pony to escape. So we take Cloud and Buttercup. Y'all take Dahomey."

"Changing horses is not enough," Winter Mary put in. "Change clothes also. Midnight, take my brother's vest, and Eagle Eye will take your hat and coat." The others considered. The neatness of Winter Mary's idea was just right to complete the plan. From far away, and with his braids hidden, Eagle Eye would look like any colored man. And in Midnight's Denver duds, he could even pass for a cowboy.

Lou Boy tapped the ground. "Midnight and I will take this route. Eagle Eye, you know this water here?"

"Yes. There is a fork." He pointed to a spot.

"Close by are some old run-down farm buildings. A barn, a windmill. There's a dirt cellar under the house. Trust me, it's safe." Lou Boy dropped his eyes. Midnight wondered how he knew all that. He decided not to ask. Not now.

Instead Midnight asked, "What kinda time are we lookin' at?"

"Three sleeps to this fort," said Eagle Eye. "Another to

the fork in the water. We will wait two sleeps at the meeting place if no bluecoats come."

Midnight nodded. "It's gettin' dark now. We leave at first light. The sooner we do it, the sooner we get to Texas."

★ ★ ★

Packing their horses didn't take long. Midnight exchanged pants with Eagle Eye, giving up his shirt and jacket too. He pulled on the buffalo vest. Last, he removed his boots and packed them in his saddlebag.

Eagle Eye pulled up his hair and stuffed it under Midnight's hat.

"You take care of that hat," Midnight told him. "It was my pa's."

"You wore it in your escape?" Winter Mary asked.

"Yeah."

Eagle Eye touched the brim. "Then do not fear. Your—*pa's* hat will bring us safely to you in Kansas."

"We will see you there!" Winter Mary waved as Dahomey galloped off. Midnight climbed onto Cloud.

"Well, partner." Lou Boy slapped the back of the buffalo vest. "Let's ride!"

12

Midnight was worried from the moment Dahomey's flying black form disappeared in a brown dust cloud. He and Lou Boy rode until the last blush of light had faded from the sky. They rose just as the sun did and were back on the trail after a meal of sardines and crackers.

They rode across a hard, almost flat prairie splashed with tall buffalo grass. There were hardly any shade trees around. Here and there huge yellow sunflowers stood up out of the grass, waving gently on their stems. That afternoon they spotted a small herd of buffalo moving slowly past a stand of tall, jagged rocks.

"This is mighty beautiful country," Midnight commented, slowing Cloud to a trot to look at the scenery.

"Hard to farm, though." Lou Boy and Buttercup slowed, too.

"So how come you know so much about these parts? Did you and your pa ride this way?"

"No . . . I told ya my ma died when I was just a pup. Pa couldn't drag a baby around. He left me with a family in Kansas Territory till I was six or seven, then came for me."

"So what happened to 'em? They lost the farm?"

Lou Boy nodded. "Joshua died. His wife and kids tried to hold on for a year or two. Pa and I were already at the Crazy Eight when we found out she had given it up and moved back east."

The sun began to beat down. Midnight began to sweat. He wondered how Eagle Eye could stand the buffalo hair in this heat. He wondered how the buffalo could stand it.

That night they slept in the grass under a clear, starry sky. Both Midnight and Lou Boy fell into deep, dreamless snores. It was almost dusk two days later as Midnight and Lou Boy galloped toward a tall log fence that formed the outer wall of Fort Dodge, Kansas.

"Stop!" a rough voice called out from a tiny opening somewhere near the top of the ten-foot gates. "Who goes there?"

Lou Boy pulled Buttercup to a stop a few yards away. Midnight could see the rifle barrels pointing over the logs.

"Travelers!" Lou Boy called back, glancing at Midnight. "Two cowpokes headin' back to Texas from Denver!"

"Surrender your weapons at the gate!" There was a slamming and sliding noise, then a loud creaking as one of the gates swung inward. Midnight edged Cloud forward, holding his dark hands in the air.

"I don't carry no weapon!" he said firmly. Lou Boy and Buttercup trotted alongside them. Lou Boy calmly pulled his knife out of his boot and handed it up, handle first, to the uniformed soldier.

The soldier eyed Midnight suspiciously. Midnight remembered with a start that he had on Eagle Eye's clothes.

"What's that getup? You a half-breed or somethin'?" The soldier frowned.

"Naw . . . I got captured back in Colorado by some Arapaho," Midnight answered.

"And I went in to get him out," Lou Boy added.

The soldier pulled out a pencil stub, scribbled something on a scrap of paper, and shoved the scrap at Lou Boy.

"Lucky you didn't lose your own scalp. Claim your weapon with this over at the gatehouse on your way out," he muttered. He cast another curious eye on Midnight, but didn't speak to him. Midnight knew what that was about. *Bet he's wonderin' if I'm Lou Boy's slave. Let's have a little fun. See how he acts when he thinks that I'm in charge.*

Midnight cleared his throat. "We come here to buy supplies for the rest of our ride. Can you point us to the fort store and some lodgin' for the horses?"

The soldier narrowed his eyes, not answering at first.

He decided fast to follow his duty and threw a thumb over his shoulder.

"Commissary's second building to the left, across the parade grounds. Opens at eight A.M. Stables straight ahead; mess tent's round the corner there."

Midnight nodded in thanks and smiled as they left the gatekeeper behind.

"You love keepin' those fellas guessin', don't you?" Lou Boy laughed.

"They oughta quit guessin' and treat everybody the same." Midnight walked Cloud into the wide-open doors of the stable. They paid to board the horses for the night and stepped out into the cool of early evening.

The fort was full and busy. Lou Boy spotted the big mess tent first. He threw the flap back and stuck his head in.

Midnight smelled the strange mix of bad army food and strong coffee. There were two long plank tables with benches running the length of the tent. At the far end was the food table, with two fellows in grimy aprons serving up plates.

Oil lamps gave off yellow light and cast funny shadows of the men hunched over their tin dishes. The tent was only half full, but the sound of the laughter and clanking forks rose all the way up to the ceiling.

"Pay at the other end," growled the cook, slapping meat and gravy onto a plate for Midnight. Midnight sniffed the food and rolled his eyes. Lou Boy chuckled.

"Thought you were hungry," Lou Boy said. Then he

looked closely at his own plate, trying to figure out just what vegetable he was looking at.

"Yeah, well—"

"Hey!" a friendly voice called from the front of the tent.

Midnight and Lou Boy carried their plates over. Midnight strained his eyes. He grinned in amazement. There sat four brown-skinned men, each wearing the blue-coated, gold-buttoned U.S. Army uniform.

"Well, I'll be!" Lou Boy breathed in surprise.

"Come on, sit with us, Indian brother!" One of the men motioned with his fork. "Where you on your way?"

"Texas. Huntin' for my folks. Y'all fought in the war?" Midnight forgot about the food as he sat down.

"You know it! Helped the Union whup them rebs till they cried, 'No mo!' " The shortest, chunkiest soldier stood up to shake hands with them. "Wink Lewis, private, United States Army." He grabbed Midnight's hand and pumped it as if he were pumping water.

"They call me Wink 'cause they says I moved faster'n my master could wink his eye!" he explained before anyone could ask. Wink fell back into his seat.

"Private First Class Eli George."

"Private Noah Jones."

"Private First Class O. C. Charles."

"Lou Holt." Lou Boy smiled.

"Midnight Son, cowpoke." Midnight couldn't get over what he was seeing. "Guess I never figured colored men could get in on this army thing—much less to fight for their own freedom!"

"There are lots more like us," Eli George said between bites. He didn't talk like a country fellow. Midnight saw his rough-trimmed beard and deep, wise eyes gleaming in the dim light.

"Fact is, we fought so good, the army is talkin' 'bout givin' us a cavalry unit right here in Kansas!" Wink told them.

"Whew!" Midnight shook his head. "Colored cavalry. That's somethin'!"

"Y'all plannin' on joinin' this cavalry outfit?" Midnight asked.

Wink spoke up first. "How can I pass it up? The army gave me a chance to act like a man! They give me an honest wage, uniform, food, and bed like any white soldier."

"I'll never work another field!"

"We get to ride 'cross the West!"

They all sounded ready to sign on, except for Eli. He was watching Midnight's face.

"What about you?" Midnight asked Eli again.

"Don't know yet." Eli pushed back his tray.

"What're they gonna have you doin'?" Lou Boy asked.

"Keepin' the peace with the Indians," Noah said. Lou Boy glanced at Midnight.

Midnight leaned across the table. "Listen, Eli and O. C. It might be tough for you to take, but your army's willin' to do anything to open up this territory. Are you willin' to do anything to help them out?"

"You're talkin' like you know some facts." Eli set down his coffee.

"We *do* know facts!" Lou Boy raised his voice.

Eli glanced toward the other tables and stood up. "I think we should step outside." He walked with Midnight ahead of the others and through the doors.

"Just what have you seen, Midnight?" Eli asked.

"Enough. We're travelin' with two Arapaho. The army wiped out their camp 'cause they wouldn't go along with the reservation plan."

"Midnight. All we're out to do is make sure folks follow the law."

Midnight shook his head. "You and me both know that some laws are a downright crime, Eli. The Indians only did what they had to do to save their people. Like you did."

Eli looked thoughtful. He peered at Midnight through the falling darkness.

"So, how'd a kid like you get so wise, Midnight?"

"I ain't all that wise, Eli. I've just seen a lot lately. I wish—," Midnight hesitated. "—I wish you'd think real hard about this cavalry thing."

"It's an honest job, Midnight. You and I both know they're hard to come by."

"Yeah."

"I'll keep in mind what you've said." Eli cocked his

head to one side. "And what about you? Have you thought hard about what you're doing? How safe is this trip through Kansas and across Indian Territory?"

"Safe or not, Lou Boy and I gotta be on our way in the mornin'. We haveta get to our meetin' place in a day."

Eli seemed to consider his words before he spoke next. "Before you leave, please find me." He gave Midnight a salute and strode off.

13

The next day, by the time Midnight and Lou Boy got breakfast, horses, and supplies, morning was half gone. Lou Boy checked into the gatehouse to pick up his knife.

"Lou Boy—I gotta look for Eli. He said somethin' about—"

But before he got the words out, there was Eli, on horseback in full uniform. Wink rode up beside him. Midnight noticed fully packed supply bags strapped over both horses' backs.

"Mornin', Eli, Wink. I was just goin' to look you up!"

Wink jumped right in, like he had last night. "Well, here we are, Mr. Midnight Son. We're ridin' out with ya!"

"Say what?" Lou Boy shaded his eyes from the bright sunlight as he looked up.

"Eli?" Midnight put one foot in the stirrup and swung

himself up over Cloud's back. "What's Wink talkin' 'bout? You ain't stayin' here to join the cavalry?"

Eli raised his eyebrows. "We have some leave time. Wink and I thought we'd like to take a little trip." They moved toward the gate.

The guard looked them over and swung open the gate. Eli and Wink galloped ahead. Midnight and Lou Boy caught up.

"Hold it!" Midnight brought Cloud to a sudden stop. "What're you really doin', Eli?"

"We're giving you a U.S. Army escort through Indian Territory to the Texas border."

"You're jokin'!" Midnight exclaimed.

"He's honest-to-goodness," Wink declared. "We talked it over. Eli ain't made up his mind 'bout the army yet, but he made up his mind 'bout Midnight Son."

Midnight stared at them with wonder. Eli smiled and clucked to his horse.

They rode side by side, talking. The four horses spread over the narrow road leading away from the fort.

Night had fallen when they saw dark flat roofs far ahead.

"That's it!" Lou Boy spurred Buttercup on. They came upon the ghostly buildings of the homestead. In the dark they could make out a barn with gaping doors and a falling corral fence. Close by was a small sod house with one window.

Lou Boy motioned for Midnight to leave his horse and walk up to the door with him. Once they stood on the tiny porch, they could see that the door was nailed shut and wooden slats had been fixed tightly inside the window. They walked around the house while Eli and Wink waited on horseback. No one had been inside this house in a long time.

Midnight's eyes roamed the darkness. He listened to the night.

"They ain't here, Lou Boy."

"How about some light?" Eli threw light from a torch. Midnight turned his head away from the sudden brightness. Lou Boy crossed the yard.

"Well, we can put ourselves up in the barn loft," he said over his shoulder.

Midnight looked around. He saw a tumbledown chicken coop in the shadows, and a shiver went through him.

"Lou Boy—"

"We gave each other an extra couple of days, remember?"

Midnight did remember. It was just that Winter Mary and Eagle Eye were heavy on his mind.

★　★　★

Another sunrise. Where could they be? Midnight paced the length of the narrow barn and back. Two days had passed. Lou Boy's old home felt more lonesome and deserted than before.

"Midnight! Better get out here!" Lou Boy called. Midnight rushed out into the dusty barnyard.

Dahomey was galloping up with Eagle Eye sitting tall in the saddle. Winter Mary hung on behind. She hopped off as soon as Dahomey slowed down.

"Midnight!" Winter Mary ran toward them.

She looks the same, Midnight thought with relief. He looked at Dahomey and saw that he had been well cared for. Last he noticed that Eagle Eye seemed healed.

"Soldiers are after us!" she panted. "With guns!"

Midnight spun around to look for Lou Boy and the others. Lou Boy was already saddling Buttercup.

"What happened?" Midnight shot back at Eagle Eye.

"I do not know how they found us. We tried to trick them by traveling a different way, but they are good hunters."

"How close are they?" Midnight ran his hands over Dahomey, wishing that he could let him rest.

"Close," Winter Mary answered.

Just then Eli and Wink led their horses out from behind the barn. At the sight of the uniforms, Eagle Eye slapped his hand to his bow, but Midnight grabbed his arm. Eagle Eye and Winter Mary stared at their dark faces.

"Friends!" Midnight told them.

"No bluecoats can be friends!" Eagle Eye watched them uneasily, looking them over from Eli's woolly beard to Wink's spit-shined boots.

"Buffalo soldiers!" Winter Mary exclaimed.

Midnight cocked his head. With their dark brown skin and shaggy dark hair, Wink and Eli *did* remind him of buffaloes! He shook the funny thought away.

"Which way did you come?" Wink asked Eagle Eye. "Maybe we can talk to 'em."

Before Eagle Eye could speak, a rifle shot rang a hollow answer through the buildings.

"They're coming in firing!" Eli scrambled into his saddle.

"Mount up!" Midnight shouted.

"No—this way!" Lou Boy headed into the barn. Midnight looked over his shoulder, waving for Eagle Eye and Winter Mary to follow.

"Lou Boy! What're you doin'?"

Lou Boy hurried into a horse stall at the far end. He frantically brushed back the dried hay from the floor. He uncovered a wooden door. Midnight smiled in understanding and rushed to help pull it open.

"Joshua hid the root cellar good, didn't he?" Lou Boy smiled back. "You go in with them. I'll take the horses and go with Eli and Wink to try to head off the soldiers. If it works—"

"You'll be back. I gotcha." Midnight gave Lou Boy a quick nod and stumbled behind Winter Mary and Eagle Eye down the steps into the darkness.

They could hear Lou Boy scraping the hay back over them, then the thumping of his boots as he ran away.

14

"**Whump!**" Midnight banged his head as he tried to stand up. "Ouch!" He rubbed his head and tried to make his eyes work in the blackness.

"What is this place?" Winter Mary's voice echoed.

"It is like a tomb," Eagle Eye grumbled.

"It's where they keep food," Midnight said. He put his fingertips up against the ceiling to feel his way across the space.

About six feet from the steps, his hand touched wood and it gave. There was a glimmer of light.

"What is that?" Eagle Eye crossed to him. Midnight rapped with his knuckles.

"Another door!" He pushed it again, just enough to let a sliver of light into the cellar. Now they could see a few old barrels and dusty shelves.

"If I stand on a barrel, I can get a good look."

Winter Mary pulled and Eagle Eye stooped low to push with his back.

Midnight stepped up, still holding the door. He lifted his face to stare out. There was a table leg. A spider ran across the plank floor. "Come on!" he told them.

One at a time, they crawled out. The light was shining through a back window, too high to see in or out of. Midnight tiptoed to the front door and listened. There was no more gunfire, but they could hear horses and men yelling.

"Indians? Round here?" Wink didn't lie, but he didn't volunteer anything, either.

"Search the place! What are you doin' here, cowboy?"

Lou Boy said something about the old homestead, adding that there wasn't much place to hide around here.

"Well, we better move on, then, else the trail will run cold. Where you headed, boys?" the soldiers asked Eli and Wink.

"Back to Fort Dodge," Eli said. "This cowpoke was kind enough to let us rest the horses."

"Better get goin' soon. Indians don't take prisoners."

When all seemed clear, Midnight signaled to Winter Mary. She opened the cellar door again. They waited quietly until the sound of two horses was a distant clatter.

After a few minutes had passed, they heard Lou Boy calling through the main door.

"We're here!" Midnight called back. In a short time they all were on their horses again.

"That was close!" Wink mopped sweat from his forehead. "We better get on back now to keep our story straight. Right, Eli?" Midnight looked at Eli.

"Eli?" Wink repeated.

To all their amazement, Eli shook his head at Wink and reached up to rip the army stripes off his sleeve.

"Eli—," Midnight began.

"What in tarnation are ya doin'?" Wink shouted.

"Makin' my mind up, Wink. I'm going to see that these kids get to their destination."

Wink seemed to fight his surprise and confusion. "You—you're *sure* 'bout this?"

Eli gave one short nod. "I am. I'm sorry I couldn't tell you before. I guess this just made it real clear to me."

"Well, all right then." Wink raised his arm to give his friend one last salute. Eli returned the honor. Then Wink headed his horse away from them. Eli watched with a tight jaw.

"Lead on, Lou Boy!" He finally said, bringing up the rear. Again, they rode without looking back.

★   ★   ★

Lou Boy proved his skills as a guide. They made it to Indian Territory in two days. The trip through would take a week or more. During the journey, they saw some reservations in the distance and passed some close by. Once or twice they stopped for water, or to rest the horses, but the Indians they met didn't offer more than common niceness. All the settlements seemed to Midnight to be hard, rough places to live. After riding across dry, rocky land past one sad group of tipis, Eagle Eye spat angrily onto the soil.

"This is worthless land. Not good enough to farm, not big enough for a hunt!"

"There is no happiness on these reservations," Winter Mary said, with a catch in her voice.

"What was it like before—before all this?" Eli asked. Winter Mary began telling them about the great Indian gatherings called Sundances, where many tribes met to feast and dance and give thanks together.

Midnight thought of Big Running Fox and his buffalo tale. "You must be your pa's story-keeper, Winter Mary!"

"Midnight, you can keep a good story, too." Lou Boy laughed. He pushed Midnight to talk about longhorn cattle and wrangling wild horses. Eli told dangerous and courageous stories about the war. They passed the time solemnly studying the reservations and swapping stories until the hilly banks of the Red River came into distant view some ten days later.

By that time, Midnight had begun to feel like Eli was one of them—another soul traveling through the world on his own. Eli had let them know that he gave serious thought to everything he did. His leaving the army was something he'd been going over in his mind long before the homestead. Midnight liked that. Eli was a man he could learn a lot from.

"It's hard to believe we all met up two weeks ago, ain't it?" Midnight asked Eli when it was time to part ways.

"Yes. But I tell you, Midnight Son—" Eli smiled. "I'm glad we did!"

"I don't know how to thank you proper." Midnight pulled Dahomey to a stop. "You ain't gonna miss that army uniform? It sure does speak loud."

Eli laughed. "Not as loud as two colored men, a white man, and two Indians do. I'll make my way just fine, Midnight. You go on and do the same."

"Come with us, Eli. We don't know what we'll come up against next, but—"

"No. I have people back in Georgia. I fought for a home, now I'm going to make one. I wish you the best, Midnight. Lou Boy." Eli tipped his hat to Winter Mary. "Good luck to you and your brother."

With that, he turned around. Midnight watched him for a few minutes. Eli turned once more and waved his blue hat. Midnight threw his up in the air in return. Then Eli was behind them and the Red River was ahead.

A light rain began to fall as they rode down into a shallow valley. They lost sight of the river, and the gentle wet patter turned into angry torrents.

"Can you see?" Midnight mopped water from his face, but it did no good.

"We are off the trail!" Eagle Eye shouted.

"Let's just keep together," Lou Boy yelled. "We can find our way when it slacks up!"

Hours later, the rain hadn't stopped. They passed the night huddled near their horses on what seemed to be a rise in the ground. When daylight neared, the rain slowed. But a heavy fog was swirling around them as they set out.

"Looks like we gotta stop," Lou Boy called out to Midnight, who was riding lead. The rain pounded down again.

"Ain't no shelter in sight!" Midnight stopped and blinked through the wetness. He could only see a few yards ahead. Everything looked flat and treeless.

"Wait!" Winter Mary leaned around her brother. "I hear someone!"

They all listened. It was a man's voice, yelling to his cattle. Midnight headed for the sound. The others followed closely.

The man was drenched and so covered with mud that they couldn't tell what he really looked like. He was trying to pound a fence post into the slippery ground. A whole section of the wooden fence lay toppled over and partly trampled.

"Need help?" Midnight shouted.

The man looked up. "You bet! I ain't got but a small herd left, and if they wander off to that river, I'm finished!"

"Where's your cattle, in or out?" Lou Boy asked.

"Got a few strays. I was tryin' to round 'em up when I saw this!"

Lou Boy, Eagle Eye, and Winter Mary dismounted to help with the fence. Midnight watched them tie their horses securely to the standing fence. He turned Dahomey to search for the missing cows.

"How far is the river?" he asked over his shoulder.

"Half a day's ride, in good weather," the man answered. "But the water rises quick with this kinda rain!"

"I'll find 'em!" Midnight rode off. Working was what he did best. He reached for his lariat, ready to rope the first cow if need be.

This is what I love, bein' out under the skies ridin'. Don't care if the sun's beatin' down, or rain, or even snow, long as it ain't no blizzard. Just me and the animals and the earth. What am I gonna do once I find Mama? They sure can't live like I do. And I don't know if I can stay in one place no more. . . .

He was pulled away from his thoughts by the lowing of a cow somewhere ahead. Right then, Midnight became a cowboy again. And it felt good.

The man they helped was named John, and they slept in his dry barn that night. He thanked them and fed them a bachelor's meal of beans and bacon. When they woke, the rain had ended. John warned them that the river would be too high to cross. They followed his suggestion and rode another day to the east.

The sun had decided to come out and stay. At the water's edge, Lou Boy trotted Buttercup over to Dahomey.

"There it is, partner. Texas at last!"

"Texas." Midnight stared ahead. "Seems like it took me a whole lifetime to get back here, Lou Boy. I think this is the longest ride I've ever made, and it ain't over yet."

Midnight spurred Dahomey on, back into the Red River, back into Texas. Back into his old life.

★   ★   ★

Once inside Texas, they had another six days of hard riding. Midnight couldn't think of rest now. His words were few and far between—only muttered directions that helped guide his friends along the way. When he saw the two live oak trees in the curve of the narrow road, he felt his heart start pounding fast.

Midnight gripped Dahomey's reins tightly. Lou Boy and the others slowed their horses and dropped behind. Dahomey jerked his head back angrily and came to a stop.

"Whoa, boy. Come on, now. Don't you remember this place?" Midnight slowly turned his head to look at the flat fields hugging the road and stretching away for miles.

He looked from side to side, searching for the groups of bent backs that should have been dotting knee-high green cotton plants. But there was no one. And there were no cotton plants—only acres and acres of patchy brown earth and yellowed weeds. Midnight eased up on Dahomey, hoping that his own muscles would relax, too. He wanted to tell somebody how strange this all was.

His friends seemed to think that he needed to arrive on his own; they were nowhere in sight. Midnight closed his eyes for a moment, then climbed out of the saddle. His legs were wobbly. He led Dahomey over to the edge of the field. Slowly he leaned down and pinched some of the dark soil between his fingers. It was rich and moist. So why wasn't there any cotton?

Midnight shook his head in bewilderment. Down that road, around the bend, was what he'd dreamed of for two years. Almost without thinking about it, he reached three fingers inside his jacket, between the buttons of his waistcoat. He pulled out a small packet of wrinkled brown paper. Standing tall, he carefully unwrapped the packet. Bright red, blue, and green silk ribbon glinted in the light. He smiled to himself. The first money he'd ever earned had bought this. Presents for Truth and Queen.

Midnight breathed deeply and gently folded the packet, returning it to its hiding place. He mounted Dahomey again and looked down from his dirt-streaked buckskin jacket to his dusty boots. He imagined that his face and hair were a sight, too. He glanced back to see his friends riding up fast.

"You sure you want your mama to see you lookin' like the cat drug you in?" Lou Boy wrinkled his sunburned nose at Midnight. Midnight began brushing furiously at the dirt, but it only puffed around him and settled back comfortably on his clothes. Winter Mary shooed him off with one hand.

"Go! She is your mother—she will take you any way you come, Midnight Son!"

Midnight looked thankfully at her and spurred Dahomey into a trot.

"Y'all comin'?" he called over his shoulder.

"We'll wait here a bit," Lou Boy said. "You go on ahead."

So Midnight rounded the curve alone, just as he had that night two years ago—but this time he wasn't running away. He was coming back, holding his head up high.

A worn-down toolshed leaned crazily into the road, blocking Midnight's view. He was surprised at how bad things looked. Fences needed mending. Trees and bushes were wild and overgrown. The place had never looked this run-down.

Where was everybody? he wondered in amazement. Past the shed the familiar redbrick chimney rose up to the sky, and all at once, the four square posts of the low plantation house were dead ahead. The big front windows were thrown open, curtains flapping out onto the porch. Midnight leaned to look for the footpath that wound around the rosebushes next to the house, the path toward the slave shacks.

Dahomey snorted as Midnight dismounted and tied him to the iron hitching post at the steps. Midnight ran his fingers over the hot metal. It was hammered into the shape of a horse's head.

"All right." Midnight knew that voice. It wasn't Papa, but he knew it.

"Put your arms up slow, and turn around like you scared!"

"Dan?" Midnight raised his hands, palms open, and looked over his shoulder.

"I don't know how you conjured my name, you bandit," snarled the skinny red-brown man. "But we done had 'nuff of the likes of you!"

Midnight was puzzled but calm. "It's me, Midnight Son. Lea and Pharaoh's boy."

The man lowered the ax handle he was holding just a little. "You ain't. . . ."

"Dan, you saved my life when I ran off from here! Helped me get away from Ben Greely!"

Dan's mouth flapped open and shut. "Naw." He grabbed Midnight's shoulders, reading his face for his father's eyes, his mother's nose.

"Mercy me! It *is* Midnight." Dan started laughing and crying at the same time.

"Dan . . . what you did for me—"

"Aw, boy, hush up. Look at you. You's a man! You's been free all that time?"

"Yeah."

"Hallelujah! Emma! Ca'line! Jacob!" He rattled off names. Midnight anxiously looked over Dan's shoulder, hoping to see his mother run breathless around that rosebush.

Where is she? This ain't right. How come he didn't start off callin' my papa and mama? Midnight sucked in his breath and pushed himself away from Dan.

Dan's face froze. Midnight's eyes opened wider. The

sound of his heartbeat became a roar between his ears. So loud that the cheerful noises of the welcoming brown and yellow and ebony people surrounding him sounded dull and muffled.

Dan pulled Midnight away to the side of the house. Everything was swimming in Midnight's sight: the door of the house, gaping open to darkness like the entrance to a big hole, the red paint of the old barn peeling off at him. He even thought he glimpsed Winter Mary moving past the split-rail fence near the barn. Midnight was standing still, yet everything else seemed to be moving.

"Midnight. They ain't here, son."

Midnight's head snapped back. He staggered, as if Dan had cuffed him with a fist.

He blinked and felt Lou Boy clap a hand against his back. Then Eagle Eye stepped up, leading the horses. He saw Midnight's face and frowned sideways at Dan. Winter Mary slipped carefully around them to stand between her brother and Midnight.

The noises stopped as everyone stared at the strangers. Midnight felt as if his friends had brought him some kind of power that he didn't have just seconds ago when he was alone. He began to feel stronger, steadier. Suddenly his head was clear and he found his voice.

"If they ain't here, Dan, then where?"

"Well, Lea walked off on that very road you come in on, not mor'n two, three weeks ago. We was hearin' talk 'bout the war bein' over, and—"

Lou Boy interrupted. "But the surrender happened back in April!"

Dan's eyes flashed angrily. "These white folks round here only told us when they saw fit."

Midnight frowned in disbelief, then shook his head. "You mean you thought you was still in bondage all that time? My mama and papa was still in these fields?"

"Listen here, Midnight. Round the first o' May, young master Ben, he come out to the lil' garden there, where we's all workin', an' he say we free to go. Just like that. Well, we kinda stood dumbfounded. All 'cept your mama, Lea." He stopped to swallow hard. Sweat popped out around his gray temples. Midnight wondered if the sweat came from the story, the heat, or both.

"*And?*" Midnight spoke more roughly than he meant to, but he had to know *now*.

"And Lea, she just dropped that ol' hoe she was workin' with and walked over to Truth and snatched her pickin' basket outta her hands and tossed it aside. She marched right on top of them tomato plants yonder and put her hand on lil' Queen's shoulder ovah by the house. Master Ben was still ramblin' on 'bout somethin'. That Lea, she say, 'I'll be takin' my leave, Mr. Greely. An' my payment for ten years' field labor to you, sir, is that horse my Pharaoh took for my boy Midnight!' Then she and them gals walk right off. Us all standin' here, watchin'. Lea never look back!"

At first, Midnight felt a surge of pride. Then—"Papa! What about Papa?"

Dan dropped his head. "Sold."

"*Sold?*" Midnight yelled. "When? Where?"

"Right after you run off. Master Ben guessed your papa was in on it. Powerful angry, he was. Young hothead. Up and sold Pharaoh two days later to some fella headed down to Galveston."

Midnight stormed away. "Midnight, hold on—," Dan called. Midnight brushed against the thorny rosebushes, sending buttery yellow petals fluttering around him to the ground.

He shoved his clenched fists into his pockets and let his feet lead him. They led him up the dirt footpath curling around the windowless little log cabins. Slave cabins. One. Two. Three. Four. Midnight strode by young children playing on the ground. They stared up at him with their mouths open. Five. Six. Seven. Eight. He stopped. Number eight had been their cabin.

He reached out for the closed door before him, but when his fingertips touched the worn wooden latch, he jerked them back. His father had whittled that latch.

Every strength went out of Midnight. He leaned his forehead against the door and cried. He didn't care that the children might be watching.

"Midnight." Winter Mary was standing behind him. "What will you do?" Midnight closed his eyes and pressed his head harder against the door. He wished that right now he could be strong like Winter Mary. He shrugged and faced her with a deep sigh. Winter Mary acted as if she didn't see his wet face and red eyes.

She threw back her head to peer up at the log roof. Her eyes roamed down every rough-cut log that made up the four walls. She lightly touched the plank door and finally rested her hand on the latch, just as Midnight had.

"How can people laugh inside such a small, dark space?" she said, almost to herself. Her study of the door had given him time to pull himself together. He knew she'd done it on purpose. In his heart he thanked her for that.

"Your father—he made this latch?"

"Yeah. Whenever Papa got the chance, he could carve amazin' things outta wood scraps. See, none of the others even got a doorknob!"

Winter Mary walked the length of the cabin—only a few steps.

"So you farmed for this man?"

Midnight grunted. "Pickin' cotton sunup to sundown day after day for no wages ain't farmin'!"

"You were prisoners in your own life. Just what blue-coats want to make of us."

Midnight raised his eyebrows at Winter Mary. He had never heard anybody explain slavery quite like that before.

"My mama told me one time that freedom's too precious for words. Since I broke away from here, my life has been as precious as water in the desert, precious as gold!" He paused and allowed himself to run his finger along the door latch. "I understand now. What I gotta do is find my mama and papa and tell them that." Winter Mary caught his arm.

"It would be good to rest here. Your people here, they want us to eat with them. We have not had real food in many sleeps!"

He looked down at her. "Fine. But I got a feelin' that Mama mighta headed back to the Sampson place, where me and Lady was born. She won't know how to find me, so she might go huntin' for Lady. First thing tomorrow, we're goin' east."

15

Midnight had heard Ca'line say food was scarce, yet a few hours later she laid the table with smoked ham and creamy field peas and watermelon pickles and steaming corn bread.

Lou Boy sat elbow to elbow with two white-haired, straight-backed men who Midnight remembered working inside the house. They had always worn black coats with shoes and gloves. He had never seen them smiling until now. They listened to Lou Boy spin a yarn about an ornery bull. Even Eagle Eye was enjoying the little brown boys and girls who stared at his beads and gingerly touched his buffalo vest. Winter Mary had refused to be served by anyone. Instead she was watching Emma make blackberry pies.

Dan settled down by Midnight as if he wanted to talk. "Midnight—"

"Tell me," Winter Mary interrupted, looking from face to face. "If you are free now, why do you stay here?"

Dan dropped his eyes. "We ain't got nowhere else to go."

"No jaw waggin'!" Old Jacob knocked his fiddlestick against a tin plate. "We gonna give Pharaoh and Lea's boy a proper welcome!" He lifted the stick and tapped one foot to set the beat. Music danced out from the fiddle into the air around them.

Eagle Eye reached into the pouch on his hip and pulled out a slender wooden flute. He watched Jacob's fingers fly over the strings, then closed his eyes and moved the flute to his lips.

And the music! Jacob's sound was playful. Eagle Eye's flute song was sad and lonely, a mournful bird calling for its lost mate. Jacob slowed the fiddle, then Eagle Eye picked up the flute. Soon the two players had a lively tune going.

"BLAM!" A rifle blast tore a hole in the music. Midnight dropped off his bench to the ground, sweeping two children under the table as he did. Winter Mary and Lou Boy huddled over the old men. Eagle Eye swapped the flute for his bow so quickly that Midnight didn't even see the switch. Midnight raised his head carefully. *One shot in the air. This ain't no Comanche raid.*

"Dan!" he whispered. "This has the smell of your boss man!" They scanned the darkness but saw nothing.

"Well, well!" The voice brought back bad memories—

Midnight thought of his escape two years ago. He'd only gotten a couple of miles from the plantation on Dahomey when Ben Greely caught him. Greely rammed Midnight in the head with the butt of his rifle just to teach "the runaway" a lesson. He'd made Dan nail Midnight up in a wooden box as punishment. Later, thanks to Dan, Midnight had gotten away for good.

Midnight's heart pounded with old anger. "Did I hear right that we've been graced with the presence of Midnight Son?"

Midnight stood when he heard his name. *Here I am, face-to-face with the last man who called himself my master.*

Even by the light of the bonfire Midnight could see the lines on Greely's forehead, around his mouth. They were only a few years apart in age, but Midnight was looking at an old man. Greely's eyes were sunken. His clothes hung on his body, much too big for the thin man who'd come back from war. He held the rifle in one hand, balanced against his hip. With the other arm he leaned heavily on an ivory-topped cane.

Greely eyed Midnight, too, standing a full foot taller than he had when he left. After a hot bath in the barn, his hair was combed and shining in the firelight. His clean red flannel shirt and buttoned waistcoat set him apart from the others. Sparkling near the ground were silver spurs. Midnight raised his chin slightly so that Greely had to look up to see his eyes.

Greely's cold blue stare met Midnight's blazing

one. He rotated the rifle on his hip so that the barrels were pointing at the center button of Midnight's waistcoat.

"Dan, who gave you leave to entertain this black horse thief?" He rolled his head around without moving his body, curling his lip at Eagle Eye, then Lou Boy.

Midnight felt his cheeks flush hot, and something inside him wanted to fly at this man and knock him to the ground.

"You, boy, are the reason I lost everything I had!" Greely spat the words out.

Midnight wasn't afraid of this man or his gun. Ben Greely had always been a bully and a coward. Midnight felt that the bully was holding the gun, but the coward couldn't fire it while they were face-to-face.

"I beg to differ with ya. Folks like us are the reason you had anything at all."

Greely's eyes flashed angrily.

Midnight finished, "Dan, I thank y'all. But we got places to go." He walked toward the gun, keeping his eyes on Greely. Then he walked right on past the man, past the barn, the house.

One of the little boys had snuck away to walk their horses out to the road. In silence, Midnight and his friends rode away. The leaves on the live oaks waved the only good-bye to be had. Midnight galloped around the curve in the dark one last time. He knew he would never, ever come this way again.

★ ★ ★

They covered the miles east in four days. They all had a new, unspoken purpose: to see Midnight's family together again. Neither time nor distance made a difference to any of them now.

Midnight and Dahomey led the party. Lou Boy had switched horses with Eagle Eye, so Eagle Eye and Winter Mary followed Midnight on Buttercup. Cloud and Lou Boy trailed them.

"Up there!" Midnight called back. "See that rise? We'll come up on the house right on the other side."

They cleared the top of the hill three abreast, looking down at the same time. Everything about the Sampson plantation was bigger and fancier than Greely's. The two-story house stood bright white against the blue sky. Huge round columns lined the long front porch, and a curved drive swept past the house to disappear behind thick old trees. The war hadn't touched this place.

"All I want is word about my mama, if I can get it," Midnight stated.

"This time we ride in together and out together," Lou Boy told him firmly.

"Agreed!" Eagle Eye said, giving Midnight a look that added, *"whether you like it or not!"* Midnight answered with a weary smile.

The sounds of busy life greeted them. Dogs barked. Somewhere someone was yelling at horses or mules. The fields were out of sight, but they could hear a chant from the workers ringing up over the cotton. As they approached the house, a girl with a white kerchief tied around her head turned from the flower bed with surprised eyes. She sprang to her bare feet and ran toward the back of the house.

Midnight and Lou Boy tied their horses to the same post. Midnight stood still.

"What if the trail stops right here, Lou Boy?" he said in a low voice.

"You can't think like that. You're gonna find them!"

The disappointment of Midnight's visit to the Greely place was heavy on his shoulders.

The polished front door swung open. A young dark boy with short legs and white breeches stood holding the big brass handle. He grinned at them quickly, then straightened his face to look back inside the house.

The door filled presently with a wide black hoop skirt hiding small, pointed-toe boots. Midnight looked up. He remembered those sharp blue eyes. And that face. Only now it was crinkled with age. Wisps of light hair curled out from her starched white lace cap. She stepped lightly for a middle-aged woman, coming right up to the edge of the porch. Midnight took note that she didn't even pause at the sight of them.

"I declare!" she exclaimed, clasping her hands together at her waist. "Who is this very unusual crew, Amos?" The boy grinned again. Midnight winked at him.

"Miz Sampson, you prob'ly don't recall me. I'm Midnight Son. I was born here."

She squinted at him. "Nooo, I . . ." She wrinkled her face more in thought. A look of understanding smoothed her features out again.

"Wait. Are you . . . Lea's boy?"

"I am." Midnight still doubted. Just because she had a keen mind didn't mean anything.

"Well, isn't this just amazing!" she drawled. "Lea herself came by here with her two girls not more than a week or two past!"

Winter Mary gasped and almost squealed. Lou Boy slapped Midnight on the back. Midnight tried not to give in to his growing excitement.

"Do you know where she was headed, Miz Sampson? I ain't seen her in over two years, and I'm tryin' to find her."

"Yes, I believe I might." She answered right away. Midnight blinked.

"Lea came to ask me who bought your sister Lady ten years ago when Mr. Sampson died. It was a young Louisiana man." She motioned to Amos.

"Get me my old ledger, Amos. And please ask Tildy to bring some drink and food for the travelers!" She sat in a cane chair on the porch and waved in the direction of an empty one beside her.

Midnight didn't move. After his run-in with Ben Greely, he didn't quite know what to make of Mrs. Sampson's generous ways. He glanced over his shoulder and caught Winter Mary's eye. She lifted her chin slightly, a strong, proud movement. Turning back, he raised his head, just a bit.

Then he walked smoothly up, remembering that when he was a boy, a slave never, ever, used the front steps. Always the back. He sat slowly in the chair and swept off his hat. He could look at his friends' faces, but his eyesight was as blurry as his thoughts.

"Here we are." Mrs. Sampson took a heavy, leather-bound book from Amos. She whipped out a pair of spectacles from within the folds of her dress.

Midnight focused his eyes on the yard as she opened the book. Tildy was serving the others from a tray. Pouring from a silver pitcher into glasses. Glasses.

"Now . . . ah!" Midnight looked back at Mrs. Sampson.

"Doctor Lemée. Just starting out with his new bride. He was from a town near the Red River called Natchitoches. The last I heard, she was still in his service." She closed the book.

Midnight stared at her brown eyes. He opened his mouth to thank her, but something made him reach out suddenly to touch the ledger. She never even flinched.

"How could you do it?" he blurted out hoarsely. "Don't you know what it did to us, sellin' Lady off that way?" He tried to control the rising of his voice, but the pain he still felt rang out.

Mrs. Sampson took a deep breath.

"My husband, Midnight Son, ran this place as a business. Slaves, crops, cattle, and all. You were no more than money to him."

"But it was *you* who—"

She nodded her head. "I had never owned a thing in my life. I let others guide me when my husband first died. Now I know my own mind, and I follow it. This place is still my livelihood. It's also the livelihood of every man, woman, and child who lives here."

"You mean since the war ended?"

"Since I freed them five years ago. Those who stayed own land," she told him simply.

Midnight sat back in his chair. Amos was having friendly conversation with Lou Boy and Eagle Eye. Winter Mary was coming toward the porch.

"So things can change," Midnight said quietly.

"Yes, they can." Mrs. Sampson stood up. She shifted the ledger to the crook of her arm. "Stay a few days, if you like. Replenish your supplies from our storehouse. Then you can take up your search rested."

"Th—thank you." Midnight stumbled over the words, still unsettled. Missing out on Papa and Mama was something he hadn't counted on. Just as he'd started turning that over in his head, here was a sign of Mama! A real, sure sign!

Mrs. Sampson cleared her throat. "Midnight Son, I'm sorry." She looked at him with clear, honest eyes for a second, then swished her skirts into the house. Midnight fingered the brim of his hat.

Winter Mary watched Mrs. Sampson with interest from the bottom step, then leaned to Midnight eagerly.

"You have news?"

"Mama's been here." His voice was so low it was almost gone.

"That should lift your heart!" Winter Mary sounded encouraging.

"Guess it would, if my heart didn't have so far to go," he answered, raising his face to hers.

She didn't say another word. He could tell from the tears that welled in her eyes that she knew exactly what he meant.

They stayed two days. Midnight would have pushed on if he'd been alone, but he wanted to be fair. Eagle Eye was still mending, though he wouldn't admit it. And Winter Mary was used to walking, not riding hard. Before they finally left the Sampson place, Midnight took a walk around. A wide, well-built road wound through the property. He followed it, passing the cotton that stretched across the flat fields until it met the sky miles away. Far ahead was an area of fallow land, left unplanted so long that the grass was spotted with blue-bonnet flowers. A clump of low-growing trees seemed to call Midnight with their branches.

One tree was younger than the rest. It wasn't as tall, but its leaves threw a shade over the earth around its bottom. The trunk wasn't much thicker than Midnight's own waist.

He placed his palm against the tree trunk, just as he

had done at the front door of the old cabin. It brought no memories. He felt nothing. He looked down, sliding the toe of his boot up against the tree's spidery roots.

Midnight walked to the other side of the tree. There was a small patch of newly cleared ground. Grass and weeds had been neatly pulled away. A half circle of fist-sized rocks surrounded the clean brown earth. In the center, up near the tree's roots, was a bunch of dried wildflowers. It was tied with a faded length of string and placed just so.

A memory flashed. *My lil' brother Nile is buried right here.* His stomach tightened with ache. All he could remember clearly was Papa, digging and digging.

Midnight knelt. He talked out loud to the trees, to the clouds. "I'll track this family down or die tryin', Nile. Your big brother is makin' a promise."

Midnight was quiet and thoughtful on the next leg of the trip. In two days' time they could see the levee that held back the swollen waters of the Sabine River.

This was the border to Louisiana. The levee was topped here and there by tall dense pine trees. Amos had told them to watch for a fat old pine, split by lightning and leaning toward the water. Just over the levee they would find the crossing point.

They spotted the pine right before dusk, and camped to wait for first light. Midnight woke everyone at sunrise. The clear skies now reminded him how lucky he

was, and how close he might be to the end of this journey. Winter Mary was right. It had taken a while, but his
heart was lifted.

They galloped up the levee then down to the river's
edge and splashed in, headed for the Louisiana shore.

16

After another two-day ride east they ran up against the Red River again, this time on the other end—the same mighty Red that flowed between Indian Territory and Texas. The Red River ran on through Louisiana, joining up with its big sister the Mississippi farther south.

Lou Boy and Midnight stopped side by side at the top of a high bluff of ragged red rocks and clay. The bluff jutted out over the river's muddy waters. The river seemed quiet now in the early morning. Far below, they could see a large snapping turtle soaking up sun on a fallen log at the edge of the water. Three baby turtles perched in a row beside her.

Midnight studied the turtles. Their shells were green-gray circles. They were still. *This must be some kinda sign to me! One mama turtle, three lil' babies. Like Mama and*

Truth and Queen and Lady. I'll really find 'em soon. I know it. He looked up at the sunny sky.

"They're close, Lou Boy. I can feel it."

Lou Boy was following the flow of the water with his eyes. "Amos's uncle claimed we only had a couple hours' ride from this point to Nak-Nak," he stuttered.

"Nak-i-tosh," Winter Mary pronounced carefully. "Natchitoches."

"Let's go, then!" Midnight turned Dahomey and charged down from the bluff onto the narrow trail that led to a smooth main road.

They left the river behind, passing small farmhouses and a fine plantation mansion set among pecan trees and magnolias. What Midnight noticed most were the cotton fields—at least, what was left of them. Acres and acres had been burned. Midnight shuddered, remembering Colorado. They all rode by silently. Amos's uncle had also told them that Union soldiers had come up the river, raiding cotton farms wherever and however they could. Midnight picked up speed.

They soon rode by a few scattered town buildings. The dusty road turned into a clean, wide street. Now the sights and sounds of the town came from everywhere.

"Clip! Clop! Clip! Clop!" Midnight smiled as he looked down at the bricks. He had been too busy staring at the row of buildings ahead to notice the change in the street.

It was clear that this was the most important street in Natchitoches. They trotted past a big general store with a broad wood porch and huge, plate-glass show windows. Winter Mary read out the green-painted sign.

"Kaf-fie Fred-rick's Mer-can-tile."

There were two-story buildings with narrow balconies running across the second-floor fronts. The balcony posts were fancy-curled black iron, shining against the pale yellow stone walls. Floor-to-ceiling shutters trimmed all the windows.

"Looks like lace on a rich woman's dress, don't it?" Lou Boy said in wonder.

"Never saw a town before that was *pretty*," Midnight said. "I thought Denver was somethin', but seems like it was just *big*." He now saw that they were on a high road that looked down over a low road to his left, running along another riverbank.

This smaller body of water was dotted with all kinds of little boats, and the riverbank was crowded with stalls and booths and people.

"That looks like some kind of market," Lou Boy said.

Midnight still had the big-as-sky feeling that had come over him on the bluff. Somewhere deep inside him, a tiny hope started moving.

"Let's see how to get down there," he said. "If my sister is a cook, maybe she does her buyin' here. It's still early."

They found the place where the high road forked down a gentle slope to the water. There were wagons, mules, horses, and people zigzagging through it all.

"Here is a hitching rail. It would be better if we leave the horses, yes?" Winter Mary had already hopped off

Cloud. Eagle Eye seemed dazed by everything around him. Midnight tied Dahomey carefully. He wanted to take his time. *Why rush? Maybe things will work out, maybe not.* But that little hope was stirring up a ruckus in his belly, so he just wanted to take it slow.

"Let's split up," Midnight suggested. "We can see from one end of this thing to the other. Raise a hand if anybody comes up with somethin'. Man's name is Lemée, and he's a doctor."

Midnight rubbed his palms together. They were sweaty. Probably the June heat. He headed into the crowd.

There were all kinds of people. Farmers and fishermen were selling their wares. The fish smell lifted up from the boats. There was an old yellow woman sitting with her skirts spread in a circle on the ground, weaving baskets. Her finished work was piled around her on the skirt. Midnight paused to watch her fingers work the slender reeds tightly in and out. She never looked up, so he moved on.

There was a square-jawed fellow selling sacks of fresh-ground flour and cornmeal. Next to him a tree-tall, honey-skinned man sang, "Pleeeeeze—try our tender new peas! Mouthwaterin', tongue-ticklin', tender new peeaaas!" He towered over the gray-bearded farmer who stood beside him, weighing bunches of bright green peas still in the pod. Midnight smiled.

The tree man ended his song and looked down at Midnight with laughing eyes.

"Buyin' fresh peas today, cowboy? Got some nice early berries here, too!" He swept his arm over a basketful of plum purple blackberries. Midnight took a deep breath of the sweet air but shook his head.

"Naw, but maybe you could tell me somethin' just as good." The man eyed his boss and quickly stepped closer to Midnight with one ear cocked toward him.

"Say what, cowboy?" he said loudly. "*Two* sacks of them peas? You got it!" He began slowly measuring out peas with a wooden scoop. Lowering his voice, he spoke without looking at Midnight's face.

"What you wanna know, cowboy?"

"I'm lookin' for my sister. Come a mighty long way to find her. I believe she cooks for some doctor named Lemée."

"Lady?" The tree man's head shot up with a grin. "Why, she does favor you at that!"

Midnight's hope fairly danced. *Calm. Steady.* He forced himself to stand still.

"You know where I can find her, then?" Midnight almost begged. The tree man chuckled.

"Well, cowboy, you just turn yourself around. She be on her way right here to get some of my precious peas. I'm tellin' you, that girl can *look* at food and make it taste good. She can cook that high fancy French stuff and make a *mean* peach cobbler."

Midnight no longer heard the words. He had whipped his head around to scan the jumble of faces and colors.

Will I know her? We ain't seen each other in ten years! Will she know me? My knees are shakin'. My insides are shakin'. Oh, I hope I don't seem like a fool kid.

"Cowboy? Cowboy?" Midnight swirled back around, bumping a bushel of peas. He stooped to rake them up with his hands.

"Mornin', Early! Now what kinda commotion you got started today?" The voice was clear, light, and kind of singsong. Almost as if it were speaking a different language.

Midnight shot upright, almost spilling the peas again. The tree man was clearly having a good time.

"Cowboy." He grabbed Midnight's elbow, raising his hand. "I want you to make the acquaintance of the lovely Lady Vavasier." He drew the name out long, *Va-va-see-ay.*

There she was. Time hadn't changed her face, just filled in the once bony cheekbones so that they stood proudly above a perfect, gently rounded chin. Same smooth, pecan brown skin and wide-open eyes ready to laugh. Her head was wrapped in a yellow gingham cloth that stood up in soft rounded edges like butterfly wings. Bright gold hoops swung in her ears as she turned her head. The dress she wore was plain gray homespun. A shining starched white apron stood out against the darker color, tied tight around her waist. She wasn't a child anymore.

For a minute her eyes, dark gray like his, were wide and surprised. But only for a minute.

"M-Midnight?" Her sassy voice became small and quiet, searching. Her eyes were searching.

The hope that Midnight had let stand up inside his heart began to jump. He was tingling all over, his feet, hands, head, lips.

"It's me, Lady! It's me!"

She threw down her bundles and basket, grabbing him in a bear hug that let him know Lady Vavasier wasn't just a woman, but a powerful strong one. All his breath was pushed, squeezed, loved out. She clutched his jaws in her big hands.

"My brother! My *brother!*" she cried out, pulling at his hair and his shirt. She yanked him close again, then shoved him out at arm's length to look him up and down. They were eye to eye, because she was as tall as Midnight.

He couldn't move, just stood there, grinning until his face hurt.

"You live! *Mon Dieu!* My goodness! You live!" Lady was smiling wide, finally letting him go.

"Yeah, I live." Midnight laughed. "And I'm more alive now than I was in all of the time between us." She touched his cheek with her fingers, just like Mama used to do. A deep warmth flowed through him. A crowd of people was gathering. Midnight saw Lou Boy elbowing his way closer.

"I take it that you struck gold, huh, Midnight?" Lou Boy swept his hat off his head and bent at his waist. A rumble went through the crowd at the white boy bowing to a colored woman like she was a somebody.

She sure does carry herself like some kinda queen, Midnight thought proudly.

"Yes, indeed! Lou Boy—this here's my sister Lady. Lady, this fella's stuck with me through the hornet's nest and back."

"Pleased to meet you." Lady gripped Lou Boy's hand. Eagle Eye and Winter Mary parted the growing flock of townspeople, and another wave of mumbles rippled through.

"I am called Winter Mary. This is my brother, Eagle Eye."

Lady held out both her arms toward them. "More of my brother's travelin' companions, I know!"

Midnight stooped to pick up Lady's things. She leaned to whisper in his ear, "Come on with me, *cher.* We gonna get us some privacy from these good folk before somebody get such a shock they fall into the Cane River, yeah?"

Lady took Midnight's arm. He carried her peas and basket, winking at Early behind the stall. Winter Mary flanked him. Lou Boy took the other packages. Eagle Eye walked beside Lou Boy. As usual, his huge bow soared into the air past his head. Together they made a curious parade along the riverbank of Natchitoches.

17

"**How come that fella** called you Vavasier?" Midnight asked as they walked along.

"Because, cher—"

"And what is that you're sayin, 'cher'?"

"One thing at a time, brother!" Lady laughed, patting Midnight's arm.

"I speak a little English, little French, little Creole. *Cher*, that's like sayin' *dear*, in the Creole way. Tante Janette, the cook at the Lemée house, she raised me and taught me all she know about food. She is Creole. And my name? Well." She held her left hand up to Midnight's nose. On the fourth finger was a wide, hammered gold band.

"I got a husband!"

"What?" Midnight's mouth gaped open. "This is too much! You grown, I know that. But you speakin' French and all and *married*? When?"

"Oh, not long. Since Christmastime. Wait till you meet him. Philmare Vavasier! He is a freeman. Never been nobody's slave. Comes from down New Orleans way. He is the best furniture maker in North Louisiana."

"He must be some kinda man to deserve a wife like you." Midnight pointed out the horses.

"Oh, *cher*, you got a fine horse!" Lady stroked the side of Dahomey's head. She reached inside the basket and pulled out a carrot, breaking it into pieces. Dahomey sniffed at it, then greedily lapped it off her open hand. "We friends for life, now, you know." She looked at her brother.

"You look so good to me, Midnight Son, that I could just eat you up!"

"Save some for Mama!" He laughed.

"Mama!" Lady's eyes were wide again. "Let me tell *you!*"

"What about Mama?" Midnight asked anxiously. "I went to the Greely place, but she was gone. Made it to the Sampson place and she had been there and gone. You mean to say you *seen* her?"

"No, no, no. Come this way." Lady reached to take Winter Mary's hand as they climbed the hill at this end of the riverbank. When they stood on the main street again, Lady looked back for Lou Boy and Eagle Eye. They were coming with their horses.

"Mama sent me word." She stopped in the shade of a very old oak tree. The branches and their thick green leaves spread over them like a giant parasol. Lady reached underneath her apron and took a neatly folded paper from a pocket in her dress.

Midnight snatched it before he thought about the fact that he couldn't read it. Lady gave him a frowning sister look. Sheepishly he handed it back. At that moment Midnight felt as if the years separating them had never passed. He saw Lou Boy watching with a strange expression of amazement. Midnight wanted to say something to him, but Lady opened the paper.

"Listen. This came to my old employer, Dr. Lemée. I got it just last night." She looked up at them. "I don't work for him full-time now, only parties. Got my own business since freedom, cooking for who pays the most." She began to read.

Shreveport, May 31, 1865
Dear Dr. Lemée,
My name is Lea Pharaoh. As I cannot read or write, I am having a friend write this letter for me. I was formerly a slave on the Sampson plantation in Texas. My daughter Lady was sold to you ten years ago by Mrs. Sampson. I want to know if you still have her. If not, can you tell me something about her health and where she is now? I am a washerwoman trying to start a business here, so I do not have the money to come looking for her. Please send me an answer.

Yours truly,
Lea Pharaoh

Midnight reached for the paper gently this time, and Lady gave it. He touched the ink lines and loops as if he could read them through his fingertips or feel his mother.

"Lea Pharaoh," he repeated. "She took Papa's name so she could keep him with her all the time."

Lady looked alarmed. "What you mean, *cher?*"

"Papa got sold . . . 'cause he helped me escape."

"Papa, sold? You escaped?"

"Hold on—there's more. We got two lil' sisters. Truth and Queen."

"Sisters!" Lady shook her head.

"Believe me, it's a mighty long story," Lou Boy told Lady. She looked at the letter in Midnight's hands and seemed to make a decision. Gathering her packages, she spoke.

"Y'all come by my place. Tell me everything while I feed you. My Philmare comes for his noon meal. Then we'll talk over what to do about this letter."

Midnight refolded the letter and slipped it into her apron pocket.

"I'd be mighty pleased to meet your Philmare, Lady. But there's only one thing *to* do 'bout this letter. We go to Shreveport and answer in person."

"You're right, *cher!*" Lady nodded. She took them back along a street block or two, then turned the corner. Lady stopped at a two-story building. On the bottom level was a big window with a striped barber's pole in it. The barbershop wasn't open yet. Midnight squinted to see the barber's chair and a shelf holding colored bottles. Lady passed the window to an alley running toward the back.

"There's a public stable up that hill round the way, Midnight. Y'all menfolk go on and come back to the door at the end of this alley."

Winter Mary cast her eyes back at them as Lady led her, talking all the while, into the house. Midnight saw the same look on Winter Mary's face that Lou Boy had: a pleasant puzzlement.

When Midnight knocked and opened the door, a delicious smell pulled him right on in. The biggest thing in the room was a funny-looking black stove. It sat squat next to a small brick fireplace. Already two large iron pots were simmering over a low flame. Bowls and cups and spoons were neatly stacked on a chest to one side. The center of the room was taken up by a long, wide table. Lady's packages were spilled open in the middle.

"Come on, have a seat, *cher!*" Midnight headed to a bench near the wall. Short flowered curtains fluttered over it in the warm breeze.

Midnight suddenly felt dizzy—with hunger, tiredness, and relief. His legs didn't want to hold him up anymore. He reached out to grab a small, round table. The milk jug full of flowers wobbled as Midnight wobbled.

"Midnight?" Lou Boy was pulling him to the bench.

"Sit down, brother!" Lady hovered over him.

"Get him water!" Winter Mary's voice commanded.

Midnight leaned back against the wall with closed

eyes. Somebody held a cup of cool water to his mouth. He took a sip and sat there, half dozing and half listening as Winter Mary and Lou Boy were telling his sister how they had met him. His sister was laughing.

"Midnight, eat this." Now Lady was commanding. He opened his eyes as she shoved a bowl in his hand, full of creamy red beans poured over steaming rice. Hunks of some kind of sausage lay on top. Midnight took the spoon she was holding and dug into it.

"We got a cistern out back filled with rainwater. Y'all wash up as you like. If you want hot water, I can boil some—"

"You don't have to do nothin' special for us, Lady." Midnight wolfed down the beans and rice.

"I see my brother, first time in ten years, and he says don't do nothin' special?" She rolled her eyes. "What you think, Lou Boy?"

Lou Boy grinned and scooped up a forkful of food. "I think he's plumb crazy!"

Midnight looked around. "Where's Winter Mary?" Eagle Eye raised his head toward the ceiling. Then Midnight saw the small staircase tucked in a corner of the room.

"Upstairs," Lady said over her pots. "Getting some peace away from all of *you!*"

The door rattled and was flung open.

18

"**I'm home**, *ma chérie!*" Philmare Vavasier bent to step under the door frame. His skin was the color of pale sand—not white, but far from brown. Everything about him was long. Long face with long, straight nose. Long, wavy golden brown hair brushed back to curl around his ears and neck. Long arms running down to wide hands with long fingers holding a wooden toolbox. He reached to hug Lady, then stopped short when he cast his gold-green eyes across his kitchen.

"*Sacré!* Who are these people filling up my house?" His voice was deep, but not loud. Midnight figured that Philmare was naturally a calm fellow. He was curious now, not angry. Midnight put his bowl on the table and stood up. Philmare looked at him closely. He turned to his wife with questioning eyes.

"Philmare, this is Midnight Son."

"But no!" His smile spread so wide, it ran from one ear to the other. "Ten years she dreamed after you, brother-in-law! Welcome into our humble home!" Philmare wiped his hand on his overalls front.

"Glad to meet ya, Philmare." Midnight thought Philmare was about to shake his hand, but he let go of Lady and hugged him.

"And?" Philmare kept an arm slung over Midnight as he faced everyone.

"Lou Boy, Eagle Eye . . ." Winter Mary's moccasins padded gently down the stairs. She had brushed and rebraided her short hair, and there wasn't a speck of dust anywhere on her. Midnight wondered how she'd done that.

". . . and this is Winter Mary," he finished.

"What tribe are you, *mon ami?* Sioux? Arapaho?" Philmare pulled a low stool from the fireplace and sat at the table next to Eagle Eye.

"Arapaho. You know my people!" Eagle Eye's face lit up.

"I spent some time out west a while back. I know a little about Arapaho." Philmare used the fingertips of his right hand to tap himself on the chest. Eagle Eye recognized the sign. He almost jumped from the bench, then said something in Arapaho to Winter Mary.

"You know more than you say. You and your Lady are good people. Midnight Son, he is good people."

Midnight couldn't believe it. This was the closest Eagle Eye had ever come to calling him a friend.

"Philmare, Midnight says we mustn't wait another day. We should go to Mama immediately."

Philmare pounded the table with his fist. "Yes!" Dishes rattled and silverware jumped. "We will leave by boat tomorrow."

Midnight sat forward. "Can y'all just up and leave for a coupla days like this? I know work is hard to come by."

"Midnight, that's why we are our own boss!" Lady laughed. She came and sat with them.

"Besides." Philmare's voice dropped even lower than it already was. "Family is hard to come by, Midnight Son."

"Oh, brother-in-law! We all know the truth of that!"

★   ★   ★

That evening Midnight and Lady strolled along the riverbank. A few boats had stayed the night. They bobbed up and down on the black ribbon of water. The air was thick and hot, not the dry heat of west Texas or the crisp coolness of the Rockies. Midnight breathed and moved slowly.

"So, *cher.* What else have you saved to tell me?" Lady wasn't looking at him, but up at the clear moon.

"You know it all by now, Lady."

"No. Lou Boy said how you come to be a cowboy. And Winter Mary tells me you tried to save her people—"

"That's what she said?"

"You tell me about *you*, brother."

"I used to dream about you."

Lady kept walking. She shifted her gaze from the sky to the Cane River. "Good dreams or bad?"

"Both, I guess. Sometimes it was us playin' that shadow game, remember?" She nodded, but didn't speak. Midnight went on.

"Most times it was you callin' me in the dark, callin' me to help you. To save you—and I—I just couldn't do it!" He stopped. "They took you right outta my hands, and I wanted to stop it, but I *couldn't*!" The heavy air and heavy words were pressing on him. Lady spun around and gripped his arms. She stared directly at him, past the pain of ten years.

"Midnight Son. You could not save me. You couldn't save those Indians. Sometimes there is nothing we can do until the storm is over! I cried for Mama. I could hear your laugh come out of every little boy's mouth for a long time. But *cher*, listen to Lady. The storm is finished! And look what you did. Brought Winter Mary and Eagle Eye out of that place alive. Found me. We're about to see our mother! Look what you *did*, Midnight Son!"

"It's gonna be all right?" he half-asked, half-said. Lady pinched his cheek, then reached up to pull his hat. As she touched it, Midnight saw a smile flicker at her lips. He knew she recognized it as Papa's hat, even after all this time.

"We gonna *make* it all right, Midnight Son."

★   ★   ★

The next morning Lady was up well before daylight to boil hot water for baths. Midnight and Lou Boy took turns in a big tin bathtub hidden behind a tall folding screen. Eagle Eye and Winter Mary chose to use cold water right from the cistern.

Midnight dressed carefully in his new Denver clothes. He had brushed them off and hung them on a tree in the back overnight to air out. He'd borrowed wax from Philmare to buff his boots till they glowed.

Lou Boy washed his hair and slicked it down. With his white shirt and leather vest, Midnight thought he looked like a lawman or something!

Philmare trooped in from outside, stooping again to avoid bumping his head. He was wearing his Sunday best—a black four-button suit, starched shirt and collar, and a dark blue string tie.

"*Bonjour*, brother-in-law. And Lou Boy. Good morning! We're all turned out *très bien*, very fine to meet the mama!"

Eagle Eye followed Philmare in. His hair was tightly braided, the braids wrapped with cloth and hung with beads and long feathers. The buffalo vest was brushed free of tangles and burrs. A wide-beaded band circled his arm. His leggings were so clean of mud and dust that the painted animals and symbols seemed to jump as he moved. Midnight stopped fiddling with his spurs to look.

"I am—presentable—to the mama?" Eagle Eye turned to show himself off.

"Mighty presentable." Midnight grinned.

"And what about us, gentlemen?" Lady stepped off the bottom stair, wearing a red dress with tiny buttons that marched to her waist and a wide skirt dusting the floor. Midnight saw her hair for the first time, and without the head wrap she looked like the little girl he most remembered. Tiny braids hugged her head, winding up to a small mountain of hair held up by a silver comb.

Winter Mary came down. Her dress was of pale deerskin, dropping to her ankles. It was covered with beads of every color, forming the patterns of stars and birds. That was eye-catching enough. But her hair! The braids were undone. As she walked, a wavy black fan framed her face.

"Whoa!" Lou Boy exclaimed.

Midnight was speechless. Even though Lou Boy had kidded him about it, Midnight hadn't ever thought of Winter Mary before as—*a woman.* Now he did.

"Oooo-wee!" Philmare whistled. "We look too good today, y'all! Let's go. My friend is taking us by wagon to the boat."

Lady got into the wagon first, along with two cloth-covered baskets of goodies she had stayed up all night packing. The others climbed in after her, with Philmare sitting up front beside the driver.

They bumped along the cobblestone street, headed in the direction of the bluff. But the wagon turned off to a lower road that led to a busy dock. Midnight could look up and see the red rocks where they'd viewed the river when they arrived. Philmare explained that larger boats had to stop up here because a dam blocked the Red River at this point, keeping any water traffic from sailing down directly into Natchitoches.

"Our boat is there." Lady pointed.

19

The "boat" was a small riverboat with one upper and one lower deck. It was painted white, with a sturdy rail running around all sides. The steam pipes and chimney towered above the upper deck. The flat benches were covered by a large oilcloth to stop coal dust and soot from settling over the passengers.

A group of white travelers stood near the boat, watching the last of their bags carried on. At the end of the narrow gangplank, a small bushy-haired man eyed Midnight and Philmare.

"Mornin'!" Midnight called out. "We'll be needin' six tickets to Shreveport!"

"Colored money just as good as white to me." The man hooked his fingers through the buttonholes of his jacket. "Only I ain't got but three seats left."

"But we gotta get to Shreveport today!" Lou Boy stepped up.

Philmare cleared his throat. "The ladies will take the boat, and this man will be their escort." He reached into his coat and pulled two gold coins out of a small money pouch. Midnight turned to him.

"Hold on!"

"Midnight, we'll join you on horseback. Lady has the letter. I have it all up here." He tapped his forehead and kissed Lady on the cheek.

"Until later, *ma chérie!* Winter Mary—you'll keep your eye on this Midnight Son, yeah?"

"Like a hawk." She smiled.

Midnight boarded the boat behind Lady and Winter Mary. The white travelers sat on the upper deck, shaded by the canopy. A deckhand showed them to a tiny open area at the back of the bottom deck. The boat's paddle churned around and around, spinning up a fine mist over everything. Midnight pushed some crates against the back of the cabin for them to sit on. He looked back to see Philmare's long fingers waving. Lady leaned over the rail, waving back.

The steam whistle shrieked over their heads. The boat puffed and puttered, crawling away from the dock. Lady sat, but Midnight and Winter Mary remained standing. They watched the paddle spin the water up into white foam and throw it back. A trail of ripples followed the boat. The banks of the river were full of summer green trees. All shapes and sizes clung to the clay and hung toward the water.

"Feels like we're some kinda birds, floatin' on top of the water this way," Midnight said.

"*Les canards.*" Lady shifted the baskets on her lap. "Ducks. Waterbirds, like you say."

"Ducks?" Winter Mary and Midnight repeated together.

"Oh—y'all never saw a duck?" Lady began to describe the webbed feet and quacking call. From that, they went on to talk about cougars and buffalo and people who looked like ducks and cougars and buffalo. They laughed a lot.

At the waterfront in Shreveport they climbed up the steep hill of the levee. Lady asked for directions, and they started out for the "colored" part of town. In the heat of the afternoon there weren't many people on the dusty streets. When they did pass a person leaning in the shade of a tree or a pair of businessmen talking in a doorway, heads turned to follow them.

Winter Mary rounded a corner sharply and Midnight did, too. Lady lagged behind.

"Wait, *cher!* You sure it's this way?"

"Winter Mary has only gotta hear directions once and she could find a needle in a haystack, sister!"

"It is the right way." Winter Mary came back to walk with Lady.

A few buildings down was a tiny unpainted house. Clotheslines crisscrossed the yard. A tall, broad-shouldered girl stirred a steaming cauldron with a long stick.

Catching sight of her, Lady let out a small gasp.

"*Cher*, she's the image of you."

"Truth!" Midnight dragged Lady across the street. "Winter Mary, c'mon!" He stopped with his hand on the gate.

The girl had seen them coming.

"Miss Truth! What you call yourself doin', gal?"

She eased her stick out of the water when he called her by name. Midnight didn't open the gate. He didn't want to scare her.

"Don't you know me?" He softened his voice. "Your big brother, Midnight Son?"

Something sparkled in Truth's eyes. She stared at him, loosening her grip on the stick and dropping it.

"You came back," she said, unbelieving. "Midnight! You came back!" She stood there, shaking and crying all at once.

Midnight hopped the wooden slats and strode to her in three long steps. He snatched her up in a hug. She buried her face in his neck.

"Where's Mama? Where's Queen?" Midnight asked the tight corkscrew curls.

"Mama went down the road, collectin' a load of laundry. Queenie, she's inside." Truth raised her head. "Who these ladies be, Midnight? She an *Indian*?"

Midnight put Truth down on her feet.

"Yeah. This here's Winter Mary. And this—" Lady elbowed him away.

"No fine talkin', Midnight. Hello, pretty little one. I'm the sister you never did meet before. I'm Lady."

Truth sucked in her breath and looked at Midnight. He nodded, grinning.

"I found her only yesterday. Now I found y'all, too. But where is my Queen?" Midnight leapt up the two steps at the door.

"Midnight!" Truth raced behind him.

"Queen!" Midnight's loud man call bounced around the walls of the darkened room. A frightened whimper came from a corner, giving him such a start that he stumbled backward.

"What is it?" Lady and Winter Mary rushed to his side.

"I don't know." He jerked his head at Truth. She tried to squeeze past him.

"Lemme go in first," she whispered.

"No," he said. He willed his nerves to be quiet and squinted in the dimness.

"Queen? It's Midnight Son." He saw her clutching the arms of her chair. Her round brown face was gone. She was thin. So frail, he could see her sharp knees poking under her skirt. She didn't move.

Midnight went closer and crouched. There was something about the way she looked at him. She moved her head at the sound, but not her eyes. Then he knew. Queen was blind.

Midnight stood up suddenly. For a minute his hope and his breath were knocked clean out of him.

Truth yanked him outside, leaving Lady and Winter Mary unpacking baskets.

"She kept runnin' off after you 'scaped and they took Papa away. Two times, three times. Me or Mama would find her. Last time she was gone for days. They sent men out. Found her where she fell at the bottom of some old well."

"Awww . . ." Midnight rolled his eyes to the sky, but there was no comfort there.

"When Queenie finally woke up, she couldn't see nothin', wouldn't say nothin'."

"Wouldn't?" Midnight saw a bird glide out of the clouds. He looked at Truth.

"She hears all right. Seems like she just don't have nothin' t' say no more."

He reached for Truth's hand and squeezed it. Then he set his jaw and went back into the house, straight to Queen. He bent low to speak into her ear.

"I'm back now, Queen. You hear me?" She raised and lowered her chin. "From now on, you're always gonna know where I am. You can count on that."

Small, cool fingers touched his cheek, his nose, his eyes, his mouth. She was smiling.

20

One by one, they each went to the low fence to watch for Mama. All eyes were on the steep hill to the left. It seemed to drop off to nowhere. Midnight carried Queen so easily that he could grip the fence with his free hand. He felt the splinters of the wood bite into his palm.

Winter Mary stood like a guard at Truth's side. Midnight glanced at Lady, who was standing apart. Her chin trembled—just for a second. *If my knees are weak, I know poor Lady must be a mess inside. It's been ten years for her!* He looked back at the street.

Something white appeared just over the top of the hill. Midnight threw the gate open and stepped out. It was the top of a big white bundle. A slender, black coffee hand appeared, lightly held against the bundle. Then her face, a dark egg shape. She had a long neck and wore a faded calico dress with a muslin apron. The bundle of clothes was balanced on her head. She seemed to be inside her own thoughts, not seeing what was ahead.

Midnight swallowed hard. "You stay with Winter Mary. Mama's comin'." He put his sister into Winter Mary's arms with care and started walking. The blazing Louisiana sun burned right through his hat to his mind, through his heart to his feet. But there was no pain. A cool peace came over him.

"Mama." She came back from her faraway world at the sound of his voice and stopped. Her eyes drank him up. Her lips parted, just a bit.

"Midnight Son!" Midnight reached to slide the bundle away from her, shifting it under his arm. It was heavy as a young calf. His mother hadn't taken her eyes off him. She had never been that much of a hugging, kissing person, even with her own family. Midnight bowed his head like a little boy when she raised a trembling hand to touch the kerchief he wore twisted at his neck. On the night of his escape she had ripped the edge of her dress off and tied it there, around Midnight's throat.

"You keep me with you all this time, my Midnight Son?"

"Always, Mama."

Midnight couldn't speak up again, his heart was so full. With his mother, he knew he didn't have to.

"You look good," was what she said, and she put her hand lightly on his arm to complete the walk. Then she stopped again, snatching her hand away. This time when she spoke, her voice shook. "How you find me, Midnight?"

Midnight grinned. Lady burst through the gate and ran down the street toward them like a child. Mama rocked a little on her feet. Midnight dropped the bundle just as her legs gave way. She plopped down weakly on the clothes as Lady grabbed her, sobbing. Mama held Lady with one arm while she pulled Midnight tight to her side with the other. He never did figure out how long they stayed that way in the middle of the street.

Mama insisted on washing the clothes she had brought home before she did any celebrating. Midnight started pumping and hauling water across the yard to refill the boiling pot.

"Can't a doctor do somethin' for Queen? I got some money saved."

"Doctors can't fix broke spirits, Midnight." She began sorting clothes. "Y'know, after y'all was born and I saw you with Pharaoh, I used to feel sorry for not knowin' my own papa. Now I wonder if it ain't better never to know, 'stead of losin' somebody you been lovin' on."

"You think Papa is lost for good?"

Mama twisted a soaking shirt, wringing it hard. "Pharaoh was sold ta some Galveston boatman named Shelby. He could be anywhere or nowhere."

"What do you *feel*, Mama?"

She stopped and looked up at him.

"You're no more boy child. You be a man. *I* feel what *I* feel. *You* feel that Pharaoh is alive somewhere."

Midnight had forgotten that his mother was the person who knew him better than he knew himself.

"I gotta try to find him, Mama. And I wanna stay here—"

"Then why don't you?"

"After I look for Papa, I made a vow to Winter Mary and Eagle Eye's mama that I haveta keep."

"What you promise?"

"Their mama asked me to take them into Missouri to try and find her sister."

"You will go, and then you come back to me," Mama said.

★   ★   ★

Philmare rode in before dawn the next morning on his bright gold palomino. Eagle Eye and Lou Boy had enjoyed the ride. Lady showed them all how much she knew her business. Mama's plain round table was scrubbed spotless. Mama didn't have many dishes, so Lady had piled the mounds of crispy fried chicken and buttery biscuits on the cloths she'd used to cover the food. She brought hard-boiled eggs and green beans cooked like Midnight had never seen before. She had sweet tomatoes and corn. There were two lemony pound cakes and some flat cookies she called tea cakes. Philmare had stopped at the river on his way, bringing fish and some funny-looking shellfish called crawfish. The fish were fried and the crawfish came to the table cooked in a mouth-watering stew with some of the tomatoes.

Even Queen seemed to eat with pleasure, especially since the visitors all took turns waiting on her. Midnight could tell that Mama was well pleased. The more they ate, the more Lady cooked.

"How long can she keep this up, Philmare?" Midnight asked between bites.

"Oh, she can go on and on, Midnight!"

"I notice you keep eating." Lou Boy laughed.

"Lou Boy, you're funny!" Truth giggled.

Midnight saw that her corkscrew curls were tied back from her forehead with a piece of rope. He snatched the little brown packet from his vest, and yards of shiny red, blue, and green ribbon fell to the floor.

Truth grabbed it up, calling out: "Sister, Midnight brought us somethin'!" She laid a ribbon across Queen's lap. Queen ran her finger along the soft satin and whispered, "Feels beautiful." Mama listened and watched.

"When I look at you, I see my mother, Raven Woman." Eagle Eye blurted out to Mama. Midnight dropped his chicken on the table. He heard both Lou Boy and Winter Mary stop talking.

Mama sat with her hands folded in her lap.

"And why be that?"

"She was dark, like you. Not Arapaho, like my father."

"Raven Woman. Strong name."

"She was a strong woman. Like you. I never think

about her people until I get to know your son. Now I am proud that Raven Woman was my mother. That I am part of people like you."

Mama said softly, "I know she be proud of you, too." Eagle Eye lowered his eyes. There was a stillness in the room.

"You know who else would be proud?" Mama smiled for the first time Midnight could remember. He had forgotten the way one cheek wrinkled on the side when she did.

"Papa would," Lady said.

"Papa. Us wanted to have land, a house belongin' to us. He used to say, 'We gonna live free with everybody else, Lea!' I never thought it would be."

"Don't give it up, Mama!" Midnight's thinking was so clear. He looked over her head at Philmare and Lady.

"Mama, I don't know how, but I'm gonna help you get some land. We're gonna make it, just like you and Papa planned."

21

Galveston was a long, narrow island connected to the Texas mainland only by boat or railroad. Midnight had gone back to Natchitoches to get Dahomey, so the ferry was their only choice for crossing. They had taken their time—nearly a week—riding through south Louisiana and Texas.

"So much water everywhere down here!" Lou Boy commented. "Bayous and rivers and lakes. Philmare, were you born swimming?"

"Almost, Lou Boy! Almost!" Philmare sat astride his palomino, watching the ferry inch slowly across the water toward them.

Midnight listened with only part of his attention. Accepting the way Queen was had given everything a bittersweet taste. He had hoped reaching Galveston would make him feel closer to Papa, more certain. *When we got to that bluff, I knew my mama was near. This land, this water is tellin' me nothin'.* He walked Dahomey back and forth along the marshy water's edge.

"Give the animal a rest!" Eagle Eye told him. "*You* walk." Midnight couldn't stay still, so he did as his friend suggested.

He had slept for almost two days at his mother's house, waking to noisy suppertimes that he wouldn't trade for anything. Lady had taken Queen back to Natchitoches when they went for Dahomey. Winter Mary, to the great surprise of her brother, announced that she wanted to stay "in the company of Ne'ina Lea." When she used the Arapaho word, Eagle Eye had looked at her oddly and turned away.

"Midnight." Eagle Eye was following on Cloud. "When do you go to this Missouri place?"

"I wanna stay with Mama awhile—" Midnight spun around to look up. "Hold it. You said when do *I* go?" Eagle Eye wouldn't meet his gaze.

"I am too much Arapaho to live as your people do. Closed inside these houses. I think I can hear my Arapaho self calling me back from far away. Now I understand your strong need to come back here."

"Yeah, but I handled it all backward, Eagle Eye!"

"No. I know that the cannons were already at the camp before we even turned back. Neither you nor I could have stopped it."

There was movement near the water. A small alligator slipped its pointed nose into the marsh and sank beneath the ripples it had made. Midnight whistled for Dahomey, keeping his eyes on the spot where the alligator had been. He took Dahomey to higher, drier ground.

"What about Winter Mary?"

"I will take her to my mother's people, but I cannot stay."

"Did you tell her any of this?" Midnight already knew the answer to that.

"Not yet."

"What are you plannin'—leavin' her? And how do you know she don't feel the same way as you do 'bout this?"

Eagle Eye shook his braids. "I cannot speak to her as a friend—like you and your sisters. We are not raised that way."

Midnight narrowed his eyes. "Look around, Eagle Eye. This world is changing right under our feet. You're the only brother she's got. And after all Winter Mary done for you to save your life, she oughta be your *best* friend! Go on and tell her what you're plannin', and listen to what she's gotta say, huh?" The ferry arrived as their conversation was over.

★　★　★

The town had been nice before the war, with two-story buildings like Natchitoches, with all the fancy trimmings. Some of the hotels and businesses still stood, empty but in good shape. Others had been burned and looted. They trotted their horses along the streets, seeing signs that a new Galveston was being built.

Midnight saw what looked like warehouses and docks. He picked up Dahomey's pace.

"Naw . . ." drawled a young white man counting boxes at one of the waterfront buildings. "Never heard of no Shelby."

"He was a boatbuilder. From somewhere round here."

The man scratched his head. "See that old white-bearded colored fella ovah there? You go ask him. He's been on these docks longer than me."

"Mister!" Midnight waved. The old man was untangling fishing nets.

"Hey, cowboy! Lookit that! Cowboys and Indians, too! What you need from an ol' sailor?"

Midnight didn't stop to think about it. "You know a boatman called Shelby? He was here in Galveston two years ago."

The old man frowned, then his face brightened. "*Captain* Shelby! Yeah!"

"Captain?" Midnight took a deep breath. "You know where he sailed to? When he comin' back?"

"Boat called the *Maude Marie*." The old man shook his head. "Ain't comin' back. Union gunboats sunk it four or five months ago."

Midnight's heart sank. He glanced at Lou Boy, clutching the reins tightly. Lou Boy's eyes were wide and unbelieving. Philmare had held back before, listening. Now he spoke.

"*Grand-père,* you work that boat?"

"Why, sure 'nuff! Got out by the skin of my old

wooden teeth, I did! Chief cook and deck swabber! I knowed all about her!" Midnight recovered.

"You recollect a tall, big-handed colored man, with scars on his back?"

The old man's eyes faded, as if he were trying hard to remember.

"Scars on his back . . . had a high name, like Prince or King . . ."

"Or Pharaoh?" Midnight asked.

"That's it! Pharaoh! Oh, but he wasn't on the *Maude Marie* when she got sunk. See, Shelby had a little side business, runnin' down to them West Indies, Nassau and such. That Pharaoh jumped ship in Nassau on a run over a year ago."

"You mean right into the water? Was he alive?" Midnight looked off toward the gently rocking boats tied to the pier.

"Don't know. Y'all friends o' his?"

"Yes, *Grand-père.* Friends," Philmare answered. The fisherman looked back to his nets.

Midnight dug his hands into his pockets. "I wanna walk the sand. See the sky Papa saw right before he left his land." The old man pointed to the beach without looking up again.

Tall sea grass disappeared as the ground flattened out to the pale yellow sand. White shells sparkled and crunched under their feet.

Midnight could hear a noise unlike anything he'd known before, a kind of low roar. The sound came and went, loud, then softer. It was the sound of the waves, the sound of the Gulf as it flowed out to the ocean beyond. Midnight had waves inside him. Small worries and big hopes rising and falling, but never stopping.

Midnight, Lou Boy, Eagle Eye, and Philmare stood shoulder to shoulder in the soft sand, staring across the sea as if the other side was in sight. As if Pharaoh would somehow sail up over the horizon with a shout and a wave. Facing them were only the blue sky sprinkled with clouds and the blue water reaching out to forever.

"This is the Great Water," Eagle Eye murmured. "The end of the world."

Midnight bent to pick up a smooth brown pebble. He pulled back his arm and threw it. They saw it fly high across the water, but it fell so far away, they couldn't tell where.

"Maybe not, Eagle Eye." Midnight strained to see the splash. "Maybe this is just the beginning."

I.S. 61 Library

D|

FIC
PAT

Patrick, Denise
Lewis.

The longest ride

BC# 30061000251710 $20.19

DATE DUE	BORROWER'S NAME	ROOM NUMBER

FIC
PAT

Patrick, Denise
Lewis.

The longest ride

BC# 30061000251710 $20.19

LEONARDO DAVINCI SCHOOL IS 61Q
98 50 50TH Ave
Corona   NY 11368